COMPLICATIONS AND

OTHER STORIES

BRIAN STABLEFORD

COSMOS BOOKS · MMIII

COMPLICATIONS AND OTHER STORIES

Published in the US by **Cosmos Books**, an imprint of **Wildside Press**
P.O. Box 301, Holicong, PA 18928-0301
www.cosmos-books.com
www.wildsidepress.com

Hardcover ISBN: 1-58715-412-9
Trade Paperback ISBN: 1-58715-411-0

CONTENTS

7. Introduction

11. Complications

39. Alternate Worlds

43. The Flowers of the Forest

64. Layers of Meaning

69. The Oedipus Effect

94. Sortilege and Serendipity

123. Skinned Alive

130. Taken for a Ride

148. Virtuous Reality

156. Wildland

INTRODUCTION

All the stories in this collection are comedies of a sort, although some are much more straight-facedly sardonic than others. "Complications", which was first published the February 1992 issue of *Amazing Stories*, is perhaps the most straight-faced of the lot. It is an exercise in speculative biology which recognises that some of the characteristics of human anatomy are arbitrary accidents of fate recalling certain idiosyncratic features of the common ancestor which all mammals—or even all vertebrate species—share. Had we been luckier in our choice of remote ancestors we might not now be stuck with a throat in which our food has to negotiate a way past the portal to our lungs, or a hind end in which our excretory and reproductive systems are so absurdly and inconveniently mixed up, but there would be little story-value in such trivial amendments as those—the one which actually features in the story is far more intriguing and rather more amusing.

The seed of "Alternate Worlds" was sown when I happened to use the term "alternate world" in front of Brian Aldiss, who took me to task for it.

"They should be called alternat*ive* worlds," he told me, primly. "Calling them alternate worlds makes it sound as if they somehow *take turns*."

I naturally took this criticism to heart and decided to make amends by writing a story in which the alternate worlds really did take turns. I called it "Alternate Worlds" and sent it off to *Interzone*—whose editor bought it but insisted on changing the title to "Minimoments", thus unwittingly defeating the whole point of the exercise. I am grateful for the opportunity to set things to rights here. The story was originally published in *Interzone* 38

(August 1990).

"The Flowers of the Forest"—which was originally published in *Amazing Stories* June 1993—is a story about the importance of keeping in touch with your roots, even if you happen to belong to a starfaring culture. As Samuel R. Delany is fond of pointing out, one of the interesting properties of the language of science fiction is that it blurs the distinction between the metaphorical and the literal, gladdening the hearts of everyone who delights in wordplay.

"Layers of Meaning", from *Interzone* 21 (Autumn 1987), is also an exercise in wordplay, which borrows the text of the most famous cartoon ever published in the British satirical weekly *Punch*. I submitted the story to Punch but it was rejected with suspicious alacrity; the magazine ceased publication shortly afterwards.

"The Oedipus Effect" and "Sortilege and Serendipity" were written for a series of "shared world" anthologies designed by Roz Kaveney, Alex Stewart and Neil Gaiman. These were inspired by the success in America of George R. R. Martin's "Wild Cards" series, which adapted comic book superheroes to a text format (but were not allowed to advertise themselves as "superhero" stories because of trademark restrictions. Roz Kaveney and her associates recognised that if fate did throw up wild talents in such abundance all the useful ones would be drained away from Britain by emigration, leaving behind a confusion of more-or-less useless ones which the Civil Service's Department of Paranormal Resources would try hard to exploit in characteristically bumbling fashion, probably operating somewhat after the fashion of a glorified temping agency. "The Oedipus Effect" appeared in *Temps* edited by Neil Gaiman & Alex Stewart, published by Roc in 1991; "Sortilege and Serendipity" was *Eurotemps*, which followed in 1992.

"Skinned Alive" was one of the earliest stories I ever wrote about the possibilities of biotechnology, which later became something of a speciality of mine, as reflected in my collection *Sexual Chemistry: Sardonic Tales of the Genetic Revolution* (Simon & Schuster UK, 1991). The story was originally published in *Weekend's Fiction Extra* in September 1978.

"Taken for a Ride"—which first appeared in *Science Fiction Age* March 1994—is another story which derives its plot-pivot from the Oedipus Effect, a philosophical notion which continues to fascinate me. (I ought perhaps to mention that it was Karl Popper, not I, who first gave it that name, although he never quite seemed to grasp the fact that self-negating prophecies are much more common and much more intriguing than self-fulfilling ones.)

"Virtuous Reality", which first appeared in *Interzone* 55 (January 1992), is one of several stories I have written which "invert" the events and themes of stories by Edgar Allan Poe. I suppose I keep on doing it because it seems to work so well as a strategy for discovering ironically interesting plots.

"Wildland" was written for a theme anthology which owes its existence to one of those golden evenings at a science fiction convention when a group of writers contrive to get an editor drunk enough to agree to a proposal they just made up on the spur of the moment. (I'm entirely innocent—I heard about it second-hand, from Dave Langford.) The original intention was to call it something gross like *Sex in Space*, but that had already been used; the editor—who obviously hadn't yet sobered up—came up with *Arrows of Eros*. The book was edited by Alex Stewart and published by NEL in 1989. Like "Complications", "Wildland" is fairly straight-faced, but just as deeply ironic; the two make a reasonably appropriate pair of book-ends by virtue of the studied quirkiness of their interest in matters of sexuality.

COMPLICATIONS

"It's a boy," said Dr. Brewer, pushing her spectacles further up the bridge of her nose so that she could monitor every nuance of her patient's reaction.

Rachel was determined to remain impassive; she was, after all, an educated woman of the twentieth century. Modern science had freed her from the agonising months of hope and anxiety which her foremothers had been forced to bear while they willed their bellies to swell, and prayed that any failure to do so was merely slowness and not the consequence of their babies' maleness; modern women had a duty to respond with mature reactions.

It seemed, though, that her disappointment showed—Dr. Brewer's scrupulous eyes narrowed a little, and the puckered lips were slightly pursed. On the other hand, perhaps it was merely the older woman's readiness to see disappointment which made her perceive it, even in features as rigid as a mask.

"Had you planned for that contingency?" asked the doctor, when it was obvious that Rachel was not going to speak.

"No," Rachel answered, shortly. "That's one of the benefits of early testing, isn't it? You don't have to make any plans until you know what to plan for."

Rachel knew that Gwenifer would not be nearly so impassive when the news was relayed to her. Gwenifer, whose understanding of the calculus of probability was unfortunately rudimentary, had convinced herself that after three boys the line was almost certain to produce a girl *this time.*

Gwenifer had been trying hard for a girl herself, without any luck at all, and had begun to suspect that there might be something wrong with her own husband, who only had a couple of years left in him before deadbirth.

"Have you any idea which course you'll be likely to favour?" asked Dr. Brewer, trying hard to make the words sound tactful.

Rachel's impassivity cracked at last; it seemed to her to be a rather indelicate question, even from a doctor. She looked away. "I'll have to talk to my family about it," she said, in a low tone. Then she looked back at the doctor, ashamed of her weakness.

Again the doctor's eyes narrowed slightly, although the effect was offset this time by the fact that her spectacles had slipped down again; the unusually narrow bridge of her nose was inadequate to keep them in place.

"Of course you will," she said. Then, suddenly seeming as awkward as her patient, she said: "But I should warn you that there may be complications to be taken into account."

Rachel felt a sudden chill. "What complications?" she asked. The ostensible purpose of the test which she had undergone was to yield an assortment of data relevant to the health of mother, husband and child. Determination of the sex of the child was supposedly only a by-product, though most women inevitably regarded it as the most important question to be settled.

Dr. Brewer held up a hand in what was presumably supposed to be a re-assuring gesture. "Please don't worry, Mrs. Hale," she said. "It's nothing life-threatening. There's no danger to you, or to the embryo."

Rachel had no difficulty subtracting two from three and coming up with the right answer. "You mean something's wrong with my husband?" she said, sharply.

"It may not be serious," Dr. Brewer was quick to say. "But we'll need to explore further. A scan will show us the full extent of the problem, and I've made an appointment for Tuesday. The overwhelming probability is that it's just a minor abnormality. Even if it's more than that, there's no possible danger to you."

Rachel had never shared Gwenifer's suspicion that there was something wrong with the line, despite Gwenifer's failure to achieve a second pregnancy. Elena was on the pill and Candida was contentedly widowed, so there . . . *real* reason to suspect that there was any hereditary defect . . . until now.

"Exactly what are you saying?" Rachel asked. When Dr. Brewer hesitated, she added: "I'm perfectly capable of understanding an explanation. I may not be a specialist but I teach General Science in the lower school. I know what all the words mean."

"The test shows that there's some kind of histamine reaction taking place in your womb," said Dr. Brewer. "Histamine is a substance secreted in response to wounds, so there may simply be a minor lesion or an ulcer of some kind, although one would expect other indications if that were the case. But it's also produced in allergic reactions, and there's a possibility that your husband might become a victim of wombshare sensitivity."

Rachel felt the hollowness of her boast that she would know what the words meant. In a vague way, she did—but now she felt an urgent need to know precisely what might be involved.

"Does that mean that my husband's allergic to his own son?" she said, awkwardly.

"No. It's your womb which could be affected. There's a possibility— only a possibility, at this stage—that the onset of pregnancy has sensitised your womb in such a way that it has begun to react against the presence of the husband, and initiate a premature detachment. It's not so very uncommon, and in two cases out of three the reaction is temporary."

"And in the other third?" Rachel asked, while she thought: *It's my fault, then—the flaw is in me.*

"In some cases, the detachment proceeds far enough to be disabling. The possibility of widowhood is remote, but males are delicate creatures . . . if you were unlucky, you'd probably be unable to become pregnant again this time round."

"But it's not hereditary, is it?" said Rachel, sharply. "It's just me—it doesn't affect my mothers-in-law?"

Dr. Brewer glanced down at Rachel's records, momentarily uncertain.

"I'm the third daughter-in-law in a line," Rachel said, quickly. We have only one child in the house, and that's from the line-mother's earlier marriage. My grandmother-in-law uses contraception, but my mother-in-law doesn't—she's been hoping to become pregnant again for some time, without any luck. She had the same test that I've just had, though, when she gave birth to my husband. Nothing showed up."

The doctor furrowed her brow. "Sometimes the syndrome doesn't become detectable until a later stage of the pregnancy," she said. "It doesn't always show up at this stage, and when we do detect

13

something—as we have in your case—a specific test is still required. Some husbands *are* much more prone to this kind of rejection than others, and yes, I'm afraid it can be hereditary. Your family doctor will be notified of these results as a matter of course, and she'll probably ask your mother-in-law to come in for a scan. If she does have the same problem, we should be able to identify it and determine the extent of the damage. How old is she?"

"Twenty-five—the same age as me," answered Rachel. She felt slightly uncomfortable as she added the second phrase. Because matchmakers almost always looked for younger recipients when their daughters-in-law fell pregnant with males the doctor would deduce—correctly—that Gwenifer's and Rachel's had been a self-arranged marriage. Rachel had shared, in her own quieter fashion, Gwenifer's strong political commitment to self-arrangement, but she still felt the slight residual sting of her mother's disapproval every time she confessed that she had made her own match.

Dr. Brewer was evidently quite unconcerned with the kind of social niceties which had obsessed Rachel's mother. All she said was: "In that case, she has all the time in the world to try again." Then, after a moment's pause for thought, she added: "If there *is* something wrong, there *could* be a hereditary element involved. You'll probably want to hear the results of both sets of tests before you finally decide, but . . . it might be as well to give us a little while to check out your child before you pass him on."

Rachel was briefly tempted to cut through the circumlocution, by saying *tank him, you mean*, but she didn't. The doctor was doing her best, in difficult circumstances, and Rachel couldn't bring herself to be rude. Anyhow, tanking was no longer regarded as disguised infanticide; modern medical science made certain that males could survive just as comfortably in a glorified aquarium as they could in a womb. Just as self-arranged marriages were gradually losing the stigma which they had once carried, so the time was coming when it would be perfectly acceptable for any woman to tank her son. It would be something which could be talked about openly at dinner-parties.

Rachel could not help but wonder whether it had all been simpler in olden times, when girls routinely concealed their pregnancies until they—and hopefully they alone—were certain whether it would be a boy or a girl. Then, if it *was* a boy, and if she should so decide, a girl might simply slip away in secret to the river, and consign her unwanted offspring to the cold mercy of the current. Of course her in-laws would *know,* but they would be forced by the iron laws of etiquette and taboo never to *admit* that they knew. Civilization and science brought greater responsibilities as well as greater opportunities.

All Rachel said, in the end, was: "Yes, I see. You can be sure that I'll think about all the options. I'll see you again on Tuesday?"

Dr. Brewer smiled then, but whether the smile signified satisfaction with her response or whether it was merely a polite conclusion to the interview, Rachel could not tell.

It's a boy, Rachel thought, as she got up to leave. *It's a boy, with complications. As if there weren't complications enough, simply because it's a boy!*

* * *

Rachel knew exactly how Gwenifer would react to the news. People who were easily annoyed were easily predictable, and the downside of Gwenifer's ardent desire to be a manager of circumstance was her violent resentment of any subversion of her schemes. Her recent promotion to forewoman hadn't helped any; she was rumoured to be a real terror on the factory floor, and she was not the kind of person to leave her work personality in the locker-room when the five o'clock hooter sounded.

Gwenifer would have cursed her luck even if the only news which Rachel had brought home had been the information that the baby would be a boy, but the ominous possibility that further bad news was to come added a deeper shade of black to her mood. Unfortunately, Rachel had to face her alone. Elena and Candida worked in the town centre and had to travel home by train; the factory, like Rachel's school, was only a few streets away.

"What is this wombshare sensitivity?" Gwenifer demanded, as though Rachel—perhaps by virtue of being a teacher of science—were personally responsible for the existence of such a phenomenon.

"I don't know much about it," Rachel confessed. "It's not mentioned in the biology textbook I use in class, but that's only for fourteen-year-olds and it's already ten years out of date."

"If I've got it, surely the doctors at the Health Centre should have picked it up years ago. It's not as if I haven't asked them why I haven't become pregnant again—I should have known better than to let them fob me off with pleas to be patient. Patient!"

"It's not supposed to be serious," Rachel pointed out. "As Dr. Brewer said, you've plenty of time to try again. Even if you have to carry your present husband to term, that's only another three or four years. Then, after the deadbirth, you could marry again. You'll only be thirty-one or thirty-two when you become fertile again."

Rachel didn't bother to point out that as a committed self-arranger, Gwenifer didn't have to worry about the fact that a woman over thirty who'd never borne a daughter wouldn't readily catch the eye of a matchmaker. Even if Gwenifer couldn't find a new mother-in-law by hook or by crook, she could still adopt—this was the twentieth century, after all, and there were plenty of healthy males in the tanks.

"But I *haven't* got the time," Gwenifer complained. "The whole point of having one's daughter early is to have some life left after she's grown up. Suppose Candida had had another girl after the boy Elena received—she'd still have been engaged in active parenting when she turned fifty. I suppose Elena will have to be tested too; there's no point in her taking the pill if she can't have another child anyhow."

Rachel shrugged. "Elena's so close to widowhood that it won't make much difference," she said. "I suppose they might want to test her, though, in case there's anything problematic about the deadbirth."

Gwenifer had already forgotten about Elena, and had found a determination to set her own troubles aside, at least for the moment. "I suppose the most important question," she said, "is what we're going to do about *your* baby. Do you have anyone in mind as a possible daughter-in-law?"

The question, posed so abruptly, made Rachel impotent with embarrassment. The fact was that she did have someone "in mind"—what else was the mother-to-be of a boy supposed to think about on a thirty minute bus-ride from hospital to home?—but having someone in mind was by no means the same thing as having a definite plan of procedure. She had not the slightest idea how the person she had in mind might react to a proposal, especially one which came directly from the mother-to-be and not from a matchmaking mother-in-law.

Gwenifer, seeing her confusion, completely mistook the reason for it. "I hope you're not expecting me to make a match *for you*," she said.

In the twenty years that she had known Gwenifer, Rachel had had ample opportunity to observe her penchant for leaping recklessly to wrong conclusions, and the corollary habit of hurling around unnecessarily hurtful remarks, but this one was too hard to bear.

"Hardly," she retorted, trying to sound scornful instead of hurt. "If I decided to throw my principles overboard at the first sign of stress, I'd look for someone who could be trusted to take the business of matchmaking *seriously*."

Gwenifer had already realised what she'd said and how it sounded. Although she wasn't much given to apologising, she knew when to retreat in haste.

"Just a joke," she lied, dismissively. "It's entirely your own business—but a mother-in-law has a right to be *interested*, don't you think?"

"Well," said Rachel, unmollified, "if you must know, the doctor advised me to think seriously about tanking him temporarily, so that they can check him over thoroughly. So there'll probably be no rush, even when the happy event falls due."

Rachel had the satisfaction of seeing Gwenifer look shocked, but it only took a few seconds for her mother-in-law to pull herself together. Gwenifer prided herself on the modernity of her attitudes.

"Will you do that?" Gwenifer asked.

"I might," Rachel told her, defiantly. "I suppose it depends whether I really have got wombshare sensitivity. If I have—and if you have too—then it would be rather irresponsible of me to go foisting the child on someone else without making certain that it was okay."

"I suppose so," admitted Gwenifer. "Does that mean . . . ?" This time, she was thinking and speaking slowly enough to abandon the question, but it didn't take a mind-reader to follow the line of argument.

"Yes," said Rachel. "For now, the news that I'm pregnant had better stay between these four walls and the covers of my medical file. It's not that I'm ashamed of what I might have to do; it's just that there's no point at all in making an issue out of it. I certainly don't want my mother to hear about it—not until everything is settled and done. Okay?"

Gwenifer shrugged. "It's your decision," she said. "Just remember— I'm your best friend as well as your mother-in-law. We've always been as close as sisters, and if we've both got this stupid syndrome, we're in the whole bloody mess *together*."

Gwenifer genuinely meant to be reassuring—her offer of support was utterly sincere, in spite of the awkward tone of her voice—but Rachel couldn't make any appropriate response. The simple fact was that she had known Gwenifer for *too* long, and had too long consented to be dominated and led by her. She had begun to wonder whether it might have been a mistake to agree to become Gwenifer's daughter-in-law, even though they had long had a tacit contract to marry. Rachel felt in need now of *real* independence, not the false kind which was insincerely thrust upon her by this childhood friend to whom she had innocently conceded control of her life. Although there was all the difference in the world between their politics and attitudes, Gwenifer and Rachel's mother were in some ways distressingly similar.

In fact, Rachel suddenly thought—while fully aware that it was a truly *awful* thought—the intervention of medical complications into their lives might turn out to be a blessing in ugly disguise. If, indeed, they *were* in this "bloody mess" together, it might easily be the wedge that would belatedly split them apart, and set her free.

* * *

As she lay in bed that night, Rachel wondered why she had never felt that sense of well-being which—according to popular romantic fiction—was supposed to descend upon a married woman the moment her husband was lodged in her womb, not deserting her until he re-emerged again at deadbirth. Did *everybody* pretend, or was she simply a freak and a misfit? She had never known whether to blame herself for being devoid of the capacity to feel what convention said she ought to feel, or whether it was simply Gwenifer's son who was mysteriously impotent to soothe her constant anxiety.

It's not a matter for blame at all, she told herself, sternly—and not for the first time. *It's a matter for self-congratulation. No high, no hangover.*

The argument made perfect sense, but she could never make it persuasive. The truth was that she *wanted* to feel the way she was supposed to feel: calm, content, fulfilled. After all, if being married didn't make one feel better, why bother? The modern-day rewards of belonging to a linear household were, to say the least, mixed. One's mothers-in-law were supposed to be good companions, and invaluable allies against all adversity—but they could also be difficult, especially if one of them was Gwenifer.

According to the biology textbook Rachel used as a teaching aid, an implanted male was supposed to release a hormone which had a slight but significant opiate effect—an effect sufficient to make the great majority of women addicted to the presence of males in their wombs. Many widows who decided not to remarry—-and more and more widows felt that they *ought* not to remarry, given that the world's population was dangerously near three billion—needed injections of a synthetic hormone to sustain them through the withdrawal symptoms which followed deadbirth. But Candida had been one of the exceptions to the rule, adapting readily enough to life without an indwelling male, and Rachel wondered whether she might now be following in her line-mother's footsteps.

Perhaps it's another hereditary factor, Rachel thought. *Another symptom of wombshare sensitivity.*

In ancient times—even today, in famine-stricken Africa and the desolate Americas—widows who had enjoyed to the full the chemical blessings of marriage had been condemned to await in feverish anxiety the birth of another boy within the family group, and then forced to compete with the nubile girls most favoured by the matchmaking mothers-in-law. It had always seemed to Rachel to be an unkind trick for Nature to play on them, but Nature had never been renowned for her kindness, and the wisdom of lore and legend insisted that the benefits outweighed the costs.

But then, Rachel thought, *it would, wouldn't it?*

She tried so hard to feel *something* that it would almost have been a relief to feel an ache or a pain: some stirring in her entrails which might confirm that her poor husband was restless in his fleshy bed, assailed by the ingratitude of her own wayward immune system.

There was nothing at all; it was as if her brain had entirely lost contact with her nether regions, as uninspired by her pregnancy as it had been by her marriage. Her thoughts were troubled, but her body seemed stubbornly, infuriatingly calm.

How her mother would have laughed, had she known of her daughter's condition! "That'll teach you, my girl!" she would have said. "That'll teach you to fly in the face of decency, and break your mother's heart!"

Unfortunately, it hadn't so far taught her anything at all, and she doubted that it would.

* * *

The sonic scan wasn't really an ordeal, and while the instruments were recording the doctors relayed the pictures to a TV set beside the bed so that Rachel could see what was going on. Dr. Brewer had to point out the tiny embryo which was her son, because it was so hard to see, but the coiled shape of her husband was unmistakable.

It gave Rachel a creepy feeling to be looking at him that way, while he was inside her. She'd seen countless pictures of the interior of a fertile womb, of course—ranging from the neat and clinical diagrams in her school textbooks to the luridly tinted photographs taken by tiny cameras mounted on careful probes which had recently been featured by the Sunday supplements—but it wasn't the same as looking into the depths of one's own body.

She realised that she had never really *seen* her husband at all, until now. The birth-and-marriage had gone very smoothly; he'd been out of Gwenifer's womb and into hers like the proverbial rat up a drainpipe, and despite all her resolutions she'd been unable to avoid looking modestly away at the vital moment. The ancient taboos still contrived to cast their gloomy shadow over modern life, and in her particular case they were aided and abetted in no uncertain terms by a mother whose attitudes were about as liberal as Pope Joan's.

The picture on the screen was rather blurred, and Rachel couldn't imagine how the consultant could deduce from such an uncertain image whether anything was subtly wrong with the implantation of her spouse, but the technician assured her that there was information enough for expert analysis. They took more smears and samples from inside her, to make sure that they had all the data available.

Afterwards, when she'd dressed, Dr. Brewer came to see her.

"The results won't be ready for a couple of hours," said the doctor. "I wondered if you'd like to take a little tour while you're waiting."

Rachel wasn't in the least confused by the vagueness of the words; she knew that the doctor wanted to take her to see the tanks. She had no difficulty in keeping her face quite straight; a few days of turbulent doubts and the contemplation of various nightmare scenarios had adequately steeled her against atavistic disgust.

"Yes," she said, levelly and sincerely. "I'd be very interested."

She found, as Dr. Brewer led her away, that even the hospital's administrators did not seem to be entirely modern in their approach to the care and keeping of unmarried males. The tanks were in the basement, deeply buried. They were between the central heating boilers and the laundry, not so very far from the mortuary.

Although it was not the sort of thing which could decently be displayed on prime-time TV, Rachel knew well enough what she would see. She knew that the males would be swimming free in a clear but viscous nutrient solution. She knew that they would be crowded together, like eels which had been captured as they swarmed and loaded into a bucket. She knew that every one of them would be marked with indelible dye in order that they could be told apart from one another, and the provenance of each one remembered.

The main tanks were, as she had expected, little different from the big aquaria at Regent's Park Zoo, although there were three dozen smaller ones not much bigger than shoe-boxes, which were reserved for infectious occupants and those under intense individual scrutiny.

The males in the big tanks ranged in length from a newborn four inches to a fully-grown foot. They were pale pink in colour, but not the same shade as Rachel's own skin, which was faintly browned by melanin. They were almost featureless, having neither mouth-parts nor sense-organs, but their skins were delicately patterned and pitted, and her educated eye could just about pick out the portals from which the mature specimens released their sperms. The codes identifying the males were marked in red: two letters and three numbers, like flight numbers at the airport.

Rachel stood and watched, while Dr. Brewer watched her.

"We've just about perfected the nutrient solution," said the doctor, eventually. "The average lifespan of a male in the tanks is 7.13 years—that's only five weeks short of the average for successful implants in healthy wombs. They still release sperms, even though they're not implanted, but the water is constantly filtered and the sperms taken out. It's unnatural, in a way, for them to spend their entire lives swimming, but they don't seem to be at all disturbed by it."

Retention of primitive traits, thought Rachel, remembering it as though from one of her college textbooks. *Vertebrate females have come a long way, and have explored many different forms—all the myriad kinds of fishes, amphibians, reptiles, birds, and mammals—but the males remain essentially similar. All the vertebrates except the placental mammals lay their eggs in liquid-filled purses, so that the male hatchlings can swim to meet and enter the bodies of the female hatchlings. The placental mammals keep their reproductive apparatus safely tucked up within their bodies, so that males need only slither out of one vagina into another, but mammalian males still retain the ability to swim.*

21

It's an understandable echo of the evolutionary process, and has nothing to do with the fact that the traditional fate of the unwanted was to be chucked into the nearest river.

She was glad that she understood. Understanding allowed her to look into the tanks without awe or revulsion, almost entirely free of the burden of dark superstitions which had so long confused human women's attitudes to their own reproductive processes.

The only thing which corrupted her equanimity with discomfort was the hugeness of the big tank and the sheer *number* of the eel-like males confined there. Science had given women a way of keeping unwed males alive, but the modern way of life encouraged women to stay single for longer periods of their lives, thus reducing the demand for the male children which—in accordance with the sociobiological logic of natural selection—had always been produced in superabundant numbers even in the days when those doomed to remain unmarried had to be fed to the fish.

In theory, all the males in the tanks were "up for adoption". In practice, nine out of ten would simply live and die without ever knowing the comforting solidity of a wife's womb. Even in these enlightened times of free choice, few women cared to get their husbands from the tank, even though such a move could give them—if they so wished—the option of not acquiring a mother-in-law, and hence a whole line-family at the same time as they acquired a husband. Even those widows most heavily addicted to the condition of marriage usually waited until they had exhausted every last hope of finding a new mother-in-law; their visits to the tanks would be covert and confidential, and they would almost always set up as line-mothers in a different town, where they were unlikely to be the subject of gossip. Some preferred to continue the synthetic hormone injections indefinitely, despite the growing evidence connecting long-term use with an increased vulnerability to cancer.

Dr. Brewer passed on to the rows of tiny tanks where individual males were lodged. Their inhabitants looked oddly pathetic in their isolation, though Rachel knew how absurd it was to wonder whether such brainless creatures might feel lonely.

"This one already has a wife waiting for him," said the doctor. "And so have these three along here. They're only in here for observation or treatment—we'll be implanting all of them within the week, provided that they come through fit and well. So, if you have a daughter-in-law in mind, and if she were willing to wait . . . you're very welcome to bring her here to see for herself . . . "

If she were willing to wait, Rachel repeated, silently. She didn't even know if the person she had in mind would be willing to hear a proposal, let alone whether she would be willing to say yes. The question of whether she might then be willing to wait for a few extra days before consummating her marriage belonged to the remoter regions of the wilderness of ifs.

"It's too soon to start thinking about all that," said Rachel, curtly. "Let's wait until we have the verdict of the tests. Even then, we'll need to wait for the results of Gwenifer's tests before we have the full picture. It was kind of you to fit her in tomorrow."

"In the circumstances . . . " said the doctor, leaving the sentence unfinished so that she could go on to the next point at issue. "I'm glad that you're taking all this so well, Mrs. Hale, but if there's anything at all that you're uncertain about, we do have a counsellor attached to the hospital who's always available for consultation. I don't know anything about your line-family, of course, but the pace of technological change is so rapid nowadays that it's not unusual for tensions to surface even in the happiest household, when issues like this are raised."

"That's quite all right," Rachel told her. "The eldest Mrs. Hale is very understanding, and my grandmother-in-law is only a few years older than Gwenifer and myself. There's no problem with any of them."

It was true, in a way. Candida and Elena would make every effort to be supportive, and even Gwenifer might not have been a problem if only Rachel had not begun to feel so utterly *smothered* by her. There was also her mother, of course—but perhaps *she* could be left out of the matter entirely; perhaps she would never need to be told. As for Vanessa . . . how could she possibly tell whether Vanessa would be a problem or not? But Rachel did not want to see a counsellor; she was twenty-five years old and she was determined that the time had come when she must stop allowing other people to make up her mind for her.

"Let's go up, then," said the doctor. "There's still a while to wait before we'll know anything more, but you've seen all there is to see here."

"I suppose I have," said Rachel. "What will it be like, I wonder, in a hundred years' time, when there are millions of them?"

The doctor looked at her sharply, but said nothing.

"It will be such a waste, won't it?" Rachel went on. "All that flesh bound up in an impotent and useless form, waiting to die before its elements can be recycled." She didn't go on. There was no point in plumbing the uncomfortable depths of the notion. But she couldn't help thinking, privately, that there was a certain hypocrisy in striving so officiously to keep these unwanted births alive in such numbers. After all, most of a male's mass was absorbed by his wife before deadbirth, so wasn't it ridiculous to quiver with shock at the thought of turning these into food, whether for fish, or cattle, or women.

In a hundred years' time, she thought, *maybe we'll really have shaken off the burden of our past—maybe we'll be truly civilized.* It was a thought, she knew, of which Vanessa would have wholeheartedly approved; Vanessa liked nothing better than speculating about future possibilities and the betterment of the human condition.

* * *

Rachel saw Vanessa on the following day, at school. Because it was Wednesday the afternoon timetable was empty, making room for the sporting activities which were supposed to add the *corpore sano* to every pupil's *mens sana*, and the science labs were quite empty. Rachel had no plans except for catching up with her marking and trying not to think about Gwenifer's trip to the hospital, but Vanessa wanted an audience on which to test out her latest idea for a science fiction story. Vanessa had lots of ideas for science fiction stories, of which only one in ten ever reached the stage of being typed up and submitted to the magazines.

"It's about this alien planet," Vanessa explained, "where the inhabitants are pretty much like us, except that the males are sentient bipeds just like the females."

"It's been done before," Rachel pointed out.

"Sort of—as a gimmick—but I want to do it properly. Complete evolutionary logic. It'll be difficult, of course, but there are dozens of insect and crustacean species which have physically-similar males and females."

"There are also social insects whose hives have queens supported by legions of sterile female workers. That's been used as a model for humanoid alien species too, but it's never really convincing."

"Maybe not," conceded Vanessa. "But think of it this way. Suppose it was just a freak of chance that the proto-chordate species which was the common ancestor of all the vertebrates had an indwelling male. Suppose that the proto-chordate species had had a free-living male instead. Then the entire evolutionary history of the vertebrates would be different, from the first fishes to the first mammals, and from the first placentals all the way through to humans. It *might* have happened that way."

"I don't think it could have," said Rachel, after a moment's pause for thought. "It's so *wasteful* to produce full-scale males as well as females, given that a male's only function is to fertilise the female's eggs. Insects tend to be profligate that way—they often produce short-lived adults whose only function is to reproduce and die—but the bigger an organism is, the less profligate it can afford to be. The energy-economics wouldn't make sense, even for reptiles of any considerable size. For mammals there'd be the additional problem of figuring out a way for your males to fertilise eggs that are retained within the female body."

"*That's* no problem," Vanessa said, dismissively. "I'd give them something like an ovipositor so that they could introduce sperms directly into the womb. Maybe I could fudge the energy-economics by giving the male some extra functions as well as fertilisation—I don't know what, but I'll think of something. I can argue that the system would enhance the power of natural selection, because a free-living male would be able to impregnate dozens of females, so that males could compete against one another for the privilege. Only the best would breed. That might be more efficient than our system, because even the fittest of our females rarely have more than two or three husbands—unless you believe in all those old demigoddesses who effortlessly went through nine or ten, and continued bearing daughters into their nineties."

"Even if you reckon that as an advantage," Rachel pointed out, "there'd be all kinds of compensating disadvantages. All these free-living males would put a terrible strain on resources, even if women only kept the best of them around. Think of all the extra work that would need to be done to feed and support them! It's surely much more efficient to have a population consisting entirely of child-bearers. Then again, humans seem to have been so successful as a species because of the way we form strong bonds between individuals through ever-extending line-families. If males took as long to mature as females, everybody's mother-in-law would be as old as her mother, and you wouldn't have that powerful family structure—or will your males be quick to mature and short lived, despite being free-living?"

"I'm not sure," said Vanessa. "I thought I might compromise on that, and I'll have to try to figure out some other way to build in strong family groups. Maybe I'd have to make these aliens slow evolvers by comparison with us—that'd be convenient anyhow, because it's so much easier to have primitive societies in stories than technologically-advanced ones . . . maybe a species like that couldn't ever become civilized in the way we have, but that doesn't mean to say that it couldn't *exist*. I really think I can make something of the idea, Rae."

Rachel heard a desperately plaintive note in Vanessa's voice, and realised that she had been completely negative about the idea since the moment it had first been put to her. She wasn't usually like that. Usually, she would enter into the spirit of Vanessa's fictional enterprises, adding her own ideas rather than simply shooting Vanessa's down. No wonder Vanessa felt wounded.

"I'm sorry," she said, tiredly, laying down the pen which she had kept hold of throughout the exchange, as though wanting to get on with her marking. "I'm just not capable of thinking constructively today. Try me again at the weekend."

"I'll have it fully worked out by then," Vanessa promised. "Will you come to dinner Saturday—or have you got something on at home?"

"Nothing at all," said Rachel, uncomfortably aware of the fact that had things been different, she would have had to find a way to a way to seduce exactly such an invitation out of her friend—out of the friend which she could not help but have "in mind" as a possible potential daughter-in-law. Even now that she knew for sure that she *was* a victim of wombshare sensitivity, it might still be possible to think in terms of a proposal—but she did not know whether she could pluck up the courage to make such an eminently refusable offer.

I'm pregnant with a boy, Nessa, but it's a fifty-fifty chance that he might have this hereditary disease . . . he'll have to go into the tank, but it might only be for a few days. I know it wouldn't be quite the same as a traditional wedding, but do you think . . . ?

Surely it was all too awful to contemplate!

"What's up?" said Vanessa, tenderly. "It's something at home, isn't it? Is it Gwenifer?"

"She's in hospital today," said Rachel. "Nothing serious. Just tests." It was hardly a revealing admission in itself, but Vanessa already knew that Rachel had been to the hospital the day before.

"What tests?" Vanessa asked. "Is it some kind of infection you've both picked up?"

Rachel thought of telling Vanessa that it was nothing she was likely to catch, but hadn't the audacity, and didn't like to entertain the more uncomfortable implications of the notion. Instead she said: "There's a possibility that we might be suffering from something, but it's nothing life-threatening. We'll be okay. Everything will be okay."

"I won't pry if you don't want me to," said Vanessa, evidently having noticed—how could she help but notice?—that Rachel had carefully avoided telling her what it was from which she and Gwenifer she might be suffering. "But if you need someone to talk to—someone outside the line—I'm always available. You will come on Saturday, won't you?"

"Yes I will," Rachel promised. "And I'll be in a more constructive mood, I promise."

* * *

When she got home, later than usual because the bus had been held up by the roadworks near the biscuit factory, her mothers-in-law were all waiting for her. Gwenifer had the results of her test. Her husband was suffering from womb sensitivity too; he was only slightly detached and might not be entirely sterile, but Dr. Brewer had told her that the probability of her getting pregnant again by her present husband was definitely on the low side.

Elena wasn't the least disturbed by the news, and was quick to say that she didn't think it was worth the bother of having a scan and a smear test herself. Candida, on the other hand, seemed more inclined to share Gwenifer's distress; she was the head of the family, after all, and possibly the originator of the series of genetically-defective males. No one was going to say that it was her fault, but Rachel knew that she wouldn't be able to help feeling responsible. The doctor had been quick to confirm that Marianne—Candida's daughter from her previous marriage—couldn't possibly be affected, but that news could do little to lighten the house-mother's burden.

"I'm very sorry, Gwenifer," said Candida, "Elena's husband was a late baby, and it didn't seem particularly unusual that I didn't become pregnant again. The tests I had didn't show up anything unusual. They're refining them all the time, you know."

"I suppose it's really my own fault," said Gwenifer, bitterly. "I wouldn't concede control of my life to a matchmaker, so I have to take responsibility for the consequences of my own decisions."

"That's hardly fair," Elena objected. "It was *our* decision, not yours, and there was absolutely nothing wrong with it."

It was true enough, but everyone knew that if Candida had been allowed to make a match for her daughter-in-law, she would have been most unlikely to have picked someone like Gwenifer. She had admitted Gwenifer to the household readily enough, and had done her best to keep it running smoothly, but Rachel suspected that she had always regretted the fact that she could not gather together a line of daughters-in-law of her own choosing.

"There's no use bickering about who might have been at fault," said Candida, soothingly. "The only question worth addressing is where we all go from here. For the time being, Rachel is the one who has the most urgent decisions to make."

"Well . . . " Rachel began—but she wasn't allowed to finish.

"No she isn't," said Gwenifer. "*You* might not see anything urgent about my predicament, but I do. I want a divorce."

Rachel noticed that although they all turned instantly towards Gwenifer, only Marianne seemed genuinely astonished. Candida seemed hurt—though perhaps not on her own behalf—and Elena was definitely irritated, but they all knew Gwenifer well enough to know her penchant for seeking short sharp solutions to all her problems.

"I'm not sure that this is a good time to talk about breaking up the household," said Candida, "Rachel . . . "

"Rachel's a grown woman," Gwenifer cut in. "And you know perfectly well that splitting the household isn't the main point at issue. I'm not prepared to wait three or four years for a natural deadbirth when I don't have to. I want a daughter of my own while I'm still young—maybe two."

"You already have a daughter-in-law," Candida pointed out. "Have you asked her how she feels about your breaking away from this family to find another one?"

Gwenifer glanced at Rachel, but didn't let her gaze linger long enough to read anything in Rachel's expression. "Rachel and I have been fast friends since we were six years old," she said, firmly. "I assume that her first loyalty is to me, not to the household—but she's a grown woman. She can make her own decision about whether she'd rather stay here, or come with me, or become the head of her own family. Naturally, I'd prefer it if she came with me, but I'll understand if . . . "

"That's not fair," said Elena, again. "You can't just present her with a *fait accompli* and say that it's up to her to decide what choice to make. Hasn't she got enough difficulties already?"

"I . . . " Rachel began—but again she got no further.

"It's because she already has enough problems on her plate that she'll be grateful to me for removing this one," Gwenifer retorted. "How do you think she'd feel if I'd gone to her and said 'Look, Rae, I'd like a divorce but I can't go ahead unless you feel all right about it'? *That* would be adding to her confusion. This way, she just has to figure out what's best for *her*, secure in the knowledge that everyone else is looking out for her own interests."

"This is a family!" said Elena, hotly. "It's not a war of all against all, in which everyone looks after her own interests!"

"It *was* a family," said Gwenifer, "until we discovered that the links holding it together are rotten."

That brought silence down like a curtain. Marianne looked so unhappy that Rachel was quick to put a protective arm around her, and even Candida's face seemed to be drained of all colour.

Gwenifer looked about her, and said: "I'm sorry—but it is *true*, isn't it?"

"No," said Rachel, slightly surprised by the emergence of an opportunity to say something without being instantly interrupted, "it's not true. Dr. Brewer says that my child might be perfectly all right—and she's sure that she can find out one way or another, given a few days to observe him in a holding tank."

"And what will *that* solve?" countered Gwenifer. "Even if he does pass fit, who'll take him under circumstances like those? And even if your son is all right, that won't help you to have another child, and it certainly won't help *me*. I didn't want to put any pressure on you, Rae, but I assumed that you'd be thinking along the same lines as me. We can go for our divorces *together*—we can face this whole thing together, the way we always have."

"Oh sure . . . " began Elena, but this time it was Rachel who interrupted, and would not be denied.

"By 'the way we always have'," said Rachel, "I presume you mean with you in the lead and me following meekly behind."

Gwenifer, perhaps surprisingly, was more astonished than annoyed. Rachel had half-expected the words to be thrown back at her, in contemptuous agreement, but Gwenifer only shook her head, as though she were unable to believe in her faithful friend's new-found ingratitude.

"If this kind of argument is the only way that we can handle our affairs," said Candida, quietly, "then Gwenifer is quite right. We *were* a family—but we're not any more."

"That's not what *I* want," said Elena, fiercely, "and it's not what you or Rachel wants either!"

"It's not a matter of wanting," said Candida. "Nor is it the kind of thing which can be put to a vote. It only needs one broken link to destroy a chain, and if Gwenifer is convinced that the link is broken . . . that's enough. But even if the household has to break up, we're all still here for the time being. Rachel's problems are still our problems, if Rachel wants our help in dealing with them. As Gwenifer says, she's a grown woman—but that doesn't mean that she has to go her own way, alone . . . or trail in Gwenifer's wake. Even Gwenifer can surely agree with that."

All the time she was speaking, even when she was referring to Rachel, Candida kept her eyes fixed on Gwenifer. Gwenifer wilted a little under that authoritative stare.

"All right," said Gwenifer, in the defiantly dismissive manner which was so typical of her. "I was only making *my* position clear. I was trying to *help*. Sure, let's hear what Rachel has to say."

Suddenly, all eyes were on Rachel. Earlier in the conversation, she remembered, she had twice tried to intervene in order to make her own position clear—but now that position no longer seemed as clear to her as it had.

"I don't know," she said, lamely, after a moment's hesitation. "I'll have to think about it. I can't say yet whether I want to stay, or what I want to do."

She saw Gwenifer smile, and knew what she must be thinking. *Same old Rae—never knows what to do until she's told.* Elena frowned, presumably because she had some similar thought in mind. Candida only nodded. Marianne was looking at the floor unhappily, embarrassed by the whole discussion.

"Take your time," said Candida. "We *are* your family—every one of us. You know that you can rely on us all. Whatever you decide, we'll help."

Rachel knew well enough how the assurance might be decoded. What Candida was really saying was: You can stay here with us, if you want to; you can be free of Gwenifer, if you want to; we'll look after you instead. *But I don't need looking after,* Rachel thought. *I really don't—do I?*

* * *

Things didn't get any better in the days that followed. On Thursday, Gwenifer went to the hospital to make arrangements for her divorce, and came home in a bad temper because Dr. Brewer had insisted that she see the counsellor first.

The doctor and the counsellor had both argued that as there was no conclusive proof that Gwenifer's husband *was* sterile, and as she only had three or four years to wait for a natural deadbirth in any case, the surgical removal of her husband from her womb was unnecessary and inadvisable. Gwenifer—always a very assertive champion of a woman's right to choose—had been rather rude to both of them; she had advised Rachel to find another doctor, though Rachel had no quarrel whatsoever with Dr. Brewer.

The tensions within the household were heightened by the fact that its members were pulling in every possible direction. Elena wanted the household to stay together, and kept coming up with new reasons why it should not split up. Candida seemed to be taking it for granted that there would be a split of some kind, and that Gwenifer would go, whether or not Rachel went with her. Marianne was not quite sure what she wanted or expected to happen, although she did appear to hold to the commonplace opinion that four parents were better than two, and she feared that if Elena could not maintain the *status quo* then Elena too might decide to look elsewhere for the kind of household she wanted to belong to.

Rachel found herself avoiding everyone, even Marianne. While she was at school, enmeshed by familiar routines, she shifted into a different emotional gear, but as soon as she left for home she felt that she was descending into a whirlpool of uncertainty. Her attention became firmly fixed on Saturday evening, when she could take her problems to Vanessa's flat, hopeful that it would be an oasis of calm and sanity, and perhaps a place where a solution to her problems might be found.

Alas for her hopes, she couldn't relax when she arrived at Vanessa's. Vanessa was her usual cheerful self, but Rachel simply couldn't match the mood; she was knotted up inside, and she soon realised that the knot would not begin to unravel until she gave it the vital tug. She anxiously awaited an opportunity to do what she had to do, but somehow there never seemed to be an appropriate moment while Vanessa was chattering away about the logic of her science fiction story.

Eventually, Rachel concluded that there never would be an *appropriate* moment for what she had to do, and that she would simply have to muster the courage to damn propriety and act. It was not easy, but she did it.

"I'm pregnant," she said abruptly, awkwardly holding a forkful of pasta at bay while she broke the news. "It's a boy." She had not intended to say it quite so baldly, without warning or prelude, but in the circumstances there really was no way to be delicate about it.

Vanessa, who had already talked at some length—more tediously than she could have known—about the logical problems of her hypothetical world where men were like women, could not adapt to the sudden change of subject without a short breathing space. By the time she finally said "Oh!" Rachel's forkful of pasta had been very thoroughly chewed and deliberately swallowed.

"That's why I've been such poor company," Rachel explained, apologetically. "It's caused one or two problems—at home, that is."

Vanessa started to reassure her, politely, that she hadn't been poor company, but soon stopped, and started again. "I suppose it's Gwenifer who's causing problems," she said. "Don't tell me she has some ludicrously unsuitable match in mind for you!"

"That would be too much even for Gwen," said Rachel, with a faint smile. "It's not that at all. There are complications. When the doctors did the routine tests they found out that there's something wrong with my husband—and hers, too. She's getting a divorce."

"Surgically?"

"Yes. She thinks I ought to have one as well."

Vanessa blinked. "Is that necessary?" she asked, tentatively.

"No," said Rachel. "It's just that I probably won't be able to have any more children, unless and until I marry again. Gwen's been trying for some time to have a daughter, and she's not the kind of person to tolerate obstructions getting in the way of her most cherished aims."

"Never mind what kind of person Gwenifer is," said Vanessa. "How do *you* feel about it all?"

"I don't think I want a divorce," Rachel told her, trying to sound calm but definite. "Not because I share my mother's view that divorce is a kind of murder—just because . . . well, it's not the sort of thing to do lightly, and it's not as if I'm *desperate* for a daughter. I mean . . . if Gwen hadn't been so keen, I might have gone on the pill when my husband matured, to give myself more time . . . "

Vanessa had laid down her own fork. She was looking hard at Rachel, and Rachel knew what kinds of ideas must be drifting through her thoughts. "What about the child?" Vanessa asked. "Do these complications affect *him*?"

"Possibly," Rachel admitted. "It's a straight toss-up—a fifty-fifty chance. The doctor wants me to tank him for a while, so that he can be checked out." She might have added: *but I don't know whether that's a good idea* . . . but she didn't dare. Vanessa might just take the inference that she already had a womb on line to receive the child, if it didn't go into the tank.

"That's too bad," said Vanessa, neutrally.

"It's awkward," Rachel agreed. "It would be unfortunate, even in the best of circumstances, but Gwen's determination to get a divorce as soon as possible . . . well, I could have done without an instant family break-up. A quiet week or two would have helped. Candida's being kind, of course, and Marianne's sweet, but Elena and Gwenifer are at one another's throats all the time—ridiculous really, given that what Elena actually wants is to keep Gwen in the family."

"Uncomfortable for you," observed Vanessa.

Rachel nodded. "Of course," she said, desperate to fill the emerging conversational gap with some kind of chatter, "it could never happen in your imaginary world. There'd be no families in turmoil there, would there? No cut-and-slash divorces." She was tempted to add: *no boy-pregnant women desperate with anxiety about the prospect of finding a daughter-in-law* but she didn't dare.

"It's not supposed to be a paradise," Vanessa replied, half-heartedly. "If they don't have any problems, how am I going to work up a plot?"

"You'll think of something," Rachel assured her, weakly.

Vanessa opened her mouth to say something, but it seemed as if the words became stuck in her throat. She had to fight in order to make them come out. When they finally emerged, they were infected by a stutter that Rachel had never heard before in Vanessa's voice. "H-have you anyone in m-mind as a wife for the . . . " She didn't manage to reach the end of the sentence.

Rachel wished that she had the courage to say: *Yes—you,* but she didn't. Instead, she said: "No." When Vanessa didn't say anything in reply, she felt compelled to go on. "It's very difficult, you see, with the doctor wanting to make sure that the boy's all right—and if he *isn't* . . . "

"Can I have him?" Vanessa blurted out. The stammer was gone, but she sounded frightened—as though the possibility that Rachel might refuse was quite terrifying.

Rachel felt as if she might burst into tears, but she took control of herself. "Oh Ness," she said, softly. "I'm so sorry—I just didn't know how to ask. I didn't even know if I *could*."

Vanessa understood the last remark perfectly. "We're the last people in the world to need a matchmaker," she said. She was diplomatic enough not to elaborate the observation into an insult levelled against Gwenifer. "I don't need anyone else to run my life, and you don't need anyone else to run yours."

"Not any more," said Rachel. Almost immediately, though, her euphoria clouded over. There were still complications which had to be addressed. She took another mouthful of pasta, and swallowed it hurriedly before laying the fork down. "What if he's not . . . I mean, what if he's . . . ?"

"Can we cross that bridge when we come to it?" asked Vanessa, anxiously. "Or do you desperately want it settled now? It won't hurt, will it, to take a little time to think about it?"

"No," said Rachel, gratefully. "It won't hurt at all."

* * *

It was late when Rachel returned home. While she walked the mile which separated Vanessa's flat from the house she felt truly relaxed for the first time. The dimly-lit streets were quiet, and the gloom seemed oddly comforting. Ordinarily, Rachel was a little bit afraid of the dark, because it made her feel isolated and vulnerable, but tonight she did not mind being by herself.

While she walked, she made her plans. She decided to tell Candida first, in private, what she had decided. Only then, with the decision on record, would she confront Gwenifer. It was not that she had any doubts about her ability to stick to her guns, even with Gwenifer firing verbal broadsides at her, but simply that she would be able to remain calmer if what she had to say to Gwenifer was mere repetition of what she had said to Candida.

As she had expected, Candida took it all very calmly. Candida offered no opinion of her own, nor even any advice. All she said was: "If you change your mind and decide that you want to stay here, you can—however things turn out with the boy. If all goes well, your daughter-in-law would be welcome to join us if that's what you wanted. But if you're sure that you'd rather start again, somewhere else, I understand. We'll still be friends, and we'll always be glad to see you."

If only, Rachel thought, as she went to Gwenifer's room, *it could all be as simple as that.*

Inevitably, it wasn't.

"You've done *what?*" said Gwenifer, in frank disbelief.

"I've asked Vanessa Wright to marry my son, if he's pronounced healthy," said Rachel. "She's accepted. We're going to start a new line-family, on our own."

"That's not what I planned," said Gwenifer. "I hoped that you'd get a divorce, like me, so that we could start again—just you and me, the way it always was—but even if you didn't want to get a divorce, I'd still want you with me. I'm perfectly happy to welcome your daughter-in-law into our household. Did you think I wouldn't be?"

"I thought that you were content to make your own position clear, and leave my decision to me," said Rachel, knowing perfectly well that what Gwenifer had said and what Gwenifer had intended to happen were two very different things.

"I was trying to make things *easier* for you," said Gwenifer, petulantly. "If I'd thought for one minute that you'd come up with something as silly as this ... Honestly, Rae, I don't want to be rude but can you really see your-self as a line-mother?"

"Yes," said Rachel. "Yes, I can."

"You say that now," countered Gwenifer, "but you really wouldn't be able to cope. Anyway, we've always been a team. We've *always* done things together. It was a mistake to marry Elena's son, but how could I possibly *know?* It's not the end, Rae—we have a second chance. Everybody has second chances nowadays, and we mustn't be ashamed to take them."

"The trouble is," said Rachel, quietly, "that I'm not sure I've had my *first* chance yet. I think this may be it, and I intend to take it. I'm sorry, Gwen—I know how disappointed you are—but things have become too complicated."

"Disappointed!" Gwenifer exclaimed. "It's not *me* I'm worried about—it's *you.* I've always looked after you—I can't just let you walk away, just because of some stupid sickness our husbands have."

There was something in Rachel which wanted to attack and accuse, to declare that Gwenifer had always needed *her* far more than *she* had ever needed Gwenifer; that Gwenifer needed someone to be dependent on her, someone to dominate, someone to organise, someone to listen; that

Gwenifer's fierce assumption that she was always right was a mask to hide some deep-seated insecurity . . . but she knew that it wouldn't be fair, or right, or even true. It was all much more complicated than that.

"It's what I want, Gwen," she said. "I don't want a divorce, and I don't want to be your daughter-in-law all over again if you don't happen to catch a daughter next time around. I want my son to be healthy, and I want to marry him to someone I . . . " She trailed off.

"Someone you *what?*" demanded Gwenifer, knowing full well what the answer had to be.

"Someone I love," said Rachel, finding it less difficult than she had supposed it would be actually to say the word.

"You love me," said Gwenifer, leading with her chin.

"Someone I love *more* than you," said Rachel, genuinely trying to put it as gently as she could, but realising as she spoke the words that the circumlocution made it sound even worse.

"You're mad," said Gwenifer. "Quite mad."

"Maybe so," said Rachel, insincerely. "But that's what I'm going to do." And she took care to add, even though she knew what response she was setting up: "I'm sorry, Gwen."

"You probably will be," Gwenifer prophesied, darkly. "And I shan't be a bit surprised if you are."

* * *

When the time eventually came, the birth was very easy, as male births almost invariably were. In fact, Rachel thought, as she lay on her back with her legs apart, there was more to be said for bearing a male child than popular opinion was routinely prepared to concede. Daughters made you obscenely fat, and then tried to tear you apart as they made their slow and inconvenient way to the outer world; boys just slipped out, smoothly and discreetly—and in spite of all the dirty jokes which compared the process to shitting there wasn't any *real* need to feel embarrassed about its essential pleasantness. Then again, a daughter started you on twenty years of child care, whereas a son either gained you a new helpmeet in the shape of a daughter-in-law, or vanished quietly into the waters of oblivion . . .

She watched her son slide out of her body, into the vessel which awaited him. She didn't avert her eyes, and didn't even have to make a particular effort not to.

Vanessa was there, watching with her, but not to receive the newborn into her own vagina—not yet. But when Rachel looked up from her son's pink body to her friend's blushing face, she saw hope there—some apprehension, to be sure, but mostly hope.

"We'll take a cell-sample right away," Dr. Brewer assured them. "It'll take forty-eight hours—then we'll be able to tell whether he's likely to face the same problems after implantation that his father has."

Having delivered this speech, the doctor hurried away to make good her promise. It took only a couple of minutes for the nurse to tidy up, and leave Rachel alone with Vanessa.

"You know," said Vanessa softly, "I really don't mind. I'm prepared to take the risk—it's not as if it would be the end of the world if I could only bear one child by him, and I really do want him. I want to be with *you*, you see—and this might be my only chance."

"I know," said Rachel, softly. She had already done the calculations a hundred times, and knew what all the alternatives were, if this marriage didn't take place. Five years to deadbirth . . . and then what? Take a boy from the tank, immediately, knowing that it probably would be two or three years before she would become fertile again? There were other possibilities, of course. Divorce and remarriage was still an option. Then again, there was no reason why Vanessa shouldn't find a husband four or five years hence, so that Rachel might become *her* daughter-in-law if and when *she* fell pregnant with a boy . . .

But all of that was hypothetical, and all of it was complicated. Rachel wanted this marriage, but she also wanted it to be *right*. The simple thing—the one stroke of luck which was needed to make everything as right as it could be—would be for the boy to prove healthy, to break the chain of misfortune. That was what she was hoping for. She didn't want Vanessa to feel forced to volunteer to marry a defective husband, even though she was certain that Vanessa's willingness to do that was quite sincere.

Please, she asked the Fates, mutely. *Just one stroke of luck, and it will all come out right. I know it will.*

Vanessa sat and held her hand for an hour or so, and then Dr. Brewer came back, to tell them that the tests were under way.

"Can we visit him?" asked Vanessa. "Can we go to see him . . . to keep in touch?"

Dr. Brewer hesitated, and glanced at Rachel. Rachel understood the hesitation well enough. It was all very well to take a prospective mother on the tour of the tanks, in order to persuade her that she could consign her son to them with a clear conscience; the sight might have a rather different effect on a prospective wife.

"I think we should," said Rachel, positively. "It's quite all right, doctor—we're neither of us at all superstitious. I teach biology to the lower school, and Ness writes science fiction."

The doctor raised an eyebrow, but nodded her head. She did a lightning examination before telling Rachel that she could get dressed, and then she waited so that she could lead them both into the bowels of the hospital.

When she had guided them to the relevant tank, she discreetly left them alone.

Rachel stood with Vanessa, watching her son swimming lazily around in circles, for all the world as though he had been born to inhabit some warm tropical sea.

"Think how different human psychology might be, if they didn't look so much like leeches," said Vanessa softly.

"What sort of theories would an Anna Freud have come up with in your sciencefictional world?" Rachel wondered aloud, blushing slightly at the indelicate thought that after all, when you came right down to it, they were leeches, weren't they? "I suppose they wouldn't be anywhere near as bizarre as the ones ours had to produce."

"No," Vanessa agreed. "Mine would be a relatively straightforward world, psychologically speaking. All our silly taboos and superstitions, and all our horrid anxieties and guilty fears, would be quite superfluous. I still think a world like that's *conceivable*, you know. I still think things could have turned out that way, if the grandmama of all the chordates had been a slightly odder creature than she was."

Rachel stared at the reflection of her own face in the glass of the tank, contemplatively. "Men and women able to look one another in the face," she said. "Able to talk to one another, able to love one another. But it's like all Utopias—too tidy. Reality simply isn't that *orderly*."

"But sometimes," Vanessa said, "things do work out, even in our world. Sometimes, you just get lucky, in spite of all the things that can go wrong. That boy in there is healthy, Rae, I *feel* it, down here. In two days' time, I'm going to marry that boy—and I know it's going to be a *perfect* match. No complications at all."

"I hope with all my heart that you're right," said Rachel.

Fortunately, she was.

ALTERNATE WORLDS

One night, while you're fast asleep, the phone beside your bed will start to ring. You'll force your eyes open and squint at the clock; you'll be just in time to see the digits change from 3:59 to 4:00. As you reach out to pick up the receiver you'll wonder what apocalyptic purpose could possibly excuse the decision to ring you at such an ungodly hour.

"Yes?" you'll say, in a tone of voice intended to signal that this had better be important.

"Oh shit!" the voice at the other end will say. "It's true!"

"Who is this?" you'll ask, as aggressively as you can.

"You're not going to believe this," the voice will reply, "but it's you."

The sheer temerity of the claim will take your breath away. "Is this some kind of joke?" you'll ask.

"*Don't hang up!*" the voice will say, hurriedly. "Honest to God, it's no joke. I mean it—I'm *you*."

Oddly enough, the repetition of the claim won't increase your anger. Instead, it will recall to you a silly sort of conversation you sometimes used to have with your friends when you were young, where one of you would say "I'm me and you're you," whereupon the other would reply, "Oh no, *I'm* me and *you're* you." And so it would go on, *ad infinitum*—or, at least, *ad nauseam.*

"What do you mean, you're me?" you'll ask. "If you're me, who the hell am I?"

"You have to be able to understand it," the voice will tell you. "I do, and you're the same as me. Well, *almost* the same. We read the same books, and we think along the same lines—at least, I suppose we do. It's very simple: there are alternate worlds."

You'll know immediately what the voice is talking about, because the notion that the world we live in is only one of millions or billions of alternative versions which somehow exist in parallel is familiar to you from the science fiction that you've read. You'll even have heard, vaguely, of attempts by physicists to account for the annoying probability distributions in quantum physics by suggesting that whenever an electron jumps one way when it could have jumped another it really jumped both ways, but created two different worlds by so doing—so that new versions of the world are being created by the billion with every microsecond that passes, and that somewhere in the unfolding web of macroinfinitude all possibilities are contained and conserved.

In fact, you'll be so familiar with all of this that you'll feel free to issue a small correction to what the voice is saying.

"Actually," you'll say, "I prefer the term 'alternative worlds'. It's more grammatical—'alternate' makes it sound as if the worlds take turns to exist."

"Don't try to play the smartass with yourself, you pedantic bastard," the voice will reply. "That's the whole bloody point—the alternatives *do* alternate. They don't just expand like a great fan, occupying parallel spaces, because there aren't any parallel spaces for them to occupy. They take turns. The sequence of minimoments—that's the jargon term for the temporal quanta—which makes up each distinct version of the world isn't truly consecutive; all the other possible worlds have to happen in between them. What consciousness perceives as continuity has to keep making vast leaps in Real Time in order to get from one minimoment to the next—and with every second that passes that distance gets greater and greater."

"It's an interesting idea," you'll admit, grudgingly (you always were a sucker for an interesting idea, weren't you?)

"That's only the half of it," the voice will say. "The problem is that there must be a limit to the Real Time distance which continuity can jump. There must ultimately come a time when there are so many alternative worlds queued up to take their turn to exist that the connections between them will become too difficult to make. The barriers between them will begin to decay, and there'll be a brief period of temporal chaos—and then the whole thing will disintegrate. Our entire universe—*and every other possible universe*—will be smashed to minimomentary smithereens. Think about *that!*"

"Well," you'll say, trying hard to seem unimpressed, "if the world flickers out of existence, I guess we won't know a damn thing about it, so there's no need to worry about it, is there?"

"Oh yes there is," the voice will say. "It won't happen all at once, you see. The process of decay will be fairly gradual, and might take a whole second or so of measurable time; and the temporal chaos which will endure for the course of that second is potentially capable of twisting elapsed time into a kind of knot, which could play very strange tricks with our experience."

"Like what?" you'll say, sceptically.

"Like when you pick up the phone and dial your own number, you'll actually get through—to another version of yourself!"

You won't be able to help feeling an odd thrill of unease as you realise how neatly you've been led full circle, but you won't entirely like it. After all, nobody likes a smartass, even if the smartass in question is another version of oneself.

"How do you know all this?" you'll ask, trying with all your might to imply that you know full well that your mysterious caller is trying to taking the piss, and that you aren't going to fall for it.

"I got a phone ca . . . " the voice will say, interrupted in mid-word by the dialling tone.

You'll feel like a fool, because at first you'll take it for granted that your leg has been cleverly pulled by a hoaxer who was too sharp-witted to hang about while the joke went flat. Then you'll look at the clock, just in time to see the digits change from 3:59 to 4:00, and a sudden flutter of dire anxiety will take hold of you. Even then you won't believe it, because you'll be perfectly prepared, under conditions like these, to doubt your own memory. In fact, you'll probably decide that you're dreaming. But you'll know that there's one obvious way to investigate the matter further.

You'll reach out, and you'll tap out your own number on the buttons of the telephone.

Somewhere, a phone will begin to ring.

You'll wait, unbelievingly, until someone picks it up and says: "Yes." The tone of the voice will tell you quite clearly that this had better be important.

"Oh shit!" you'll say. "It's true!"

"Who is this?" the voice will inquire, aggressively.

You'll actually begin to say: "You're not going to believe this, but ... "

Then, all of a sudden, you'll realise what you're doing, and you'll be possessed by a powerful determination to get out of the loop by refusing to play the game any longer. It will suddenly occur to you with a force you never thought possible that you're a human being with free will, and that you don't have to follow any stupid script laid down by the unfolding pattern of determinism, if you don't want to.

So you'll shut up, and you'll slam down the phone.

For a second or two you'll feel really good about it. Then you'll glance at the clock, just in time to see the digits change from 3:59 to 4:00, and a peculiarly horrible feeling will begin to afflict your stomach.

The phone will begin to ring, and you'll slowly realise that it really won't matter at all whether you decide to answer it or not. One way or the other, the connection will eventually be broken, and you'll look back at the clock, just in time to see the digits changing from 3:59 to 4:00.

And the sickness in your stomach will get worse and worse and worse ...

And so *ad* . . .

THE FLOWERS OF THE FOREST

The process of reconstruction that will return my lower limbs to their normal state is under way now, but I'm still a monster for the time being, in more ways than one. It isn't just that my body is so bloated, my pelvic limbs so obscenely gross and columnar. In a month's time, when the accelerating worldship reaches the outer limits of the solar system, I'll be like everyone else again, appearance-wise—but I'll still be different *inside*, where it really counts.

The medics don't think so, of course. They take it for granted that I'll re-adapt psychologically as well as physically. The psych's opinion is that my inner sense of being different—of having fundamentally *changed*—is a straightforward reflection of the physical discomfort I feel by virtue of of being back aboard the worldship while still burdened with legs and all the other adaptations which fitted me for life in a gravity-well. She's wrong, though. I am different, and I always will be.

I'm not denying that I feel the physical discomforts, of course. On Quibor I weighed three times as much as I do now; the surface-gravity of an Earthlike planet is punishing by comparison with shipspin. In spite of the corporeal reconstruction and the long months of training, a descent even to the most benign of planetary surfaces inflicts enough wear and tear on a worldshipper's system to reduce his life-expectancy by ten or fifteen shipyears. It's not surprising that I feel like a fish out of water just now. But that has nothing to do with my thoughts, my knowledge and my soul. If physical discomfort and debilitation were all that mattered, no one would ever volunteer for a planet drop, but whenever the ship makes an orbital stop there's always fierce competition to go down.

"It's a small price to pay," Gregor said to me, when we first put in our applications. "A tenth of a lifespan, in exchange for the kind of opportunity which comes along once every three or four hundred years. It's a chance to do and see things that only one worldshipper in a million ever gets to do and see. It's a chance to touch *ground*, to return to our *roots.*"

Gregor thought of it as a straightforward price to be paid; he hadn't even bothered to calculate the risks. Neither had I. But it wasn't mere recklessness that made us do what we did. Nor was there any dereliction of duty involved in our expedition into the rainforest. We'd completed our allotted work, more than a month ahead of schedule. Everyone on the mission agreed that we were entitled to something for ourselves, and everyone took the opportunity.

If you care to look back through the records you'll find that all parties of planetary descendants behave in the same way. Nobody goes through what we went through just to compile routine reports for the Hierarchy; everyone who ever went down to a planet had his own personal agenda, his own idiosyncratic desire to make the most of an unparalleled opportunity to experience life in the raw. Gregor and I just went a little further than most of the others.

Look at the records, and you'll find that every planetdrop our ancestors ever made resulted in *someone* missing the ship. Of course, legend and popular fiction paint an entirely false picture of the *reasons* why people miss the ship. We've all seen vidromances about planetdroppers finding true love on the surfaces of beautiful and exotic worlds, and deciding to stay rather than return to the worldship when the pick-up drones arrive, but those are just fantasies. Native females, however closely they approximate to human form, are nevertheless alien. In reality, I guess, planetdroppers almost always return to their ships, unless they die, or get trapped—but what happened to Gregor was no mere accident, no commonplace disaster. There was more to it than that, and you won't be able to understand unless you can grasp the essence of the planetdropper's dream, and the true meaning of the myth of Earth and Home. You have to be able to see that the *real* reason men descend into gravity wells every time the worldship cruises through a system has nothing to do with the material and the data they bring back. All the stuff that goes into the official reports is just an excuse, just a pretence.

It's true that we sometimes learn useful things from our explorations of planetary surfaces—that our biotechnology occasionally gets a considerable boost from the discovery of some new genetic system—but that's just a bonus, not a fundamental *reason*. The attraction which planetary surfaces exert upon us is much deeper and more intimate than any merely practical motive. It's to do with what we *are*, in the core of our being. Our customs and mores, our ideas and habits of thought, are all the produce of worldship life, but we've only been worldshippers for two hundred generations; our ancestors were planet-dwellers for *twenty thousand*. Gregor was right in what he said. The process is a return to our roots, a recovery of our true selves. I may look like a monster just now, but I'm a uniquely *human* monster; this is the kind of monster that our forefathers were, in the days when they were innocent hunter/gatherers like the Quiborians—which they were for a hundred times as long as they were planet-bound progressives and worldshippers. People who apply to be planetdroppers aren't just volunteering for a nasty but necessary *job*. Gregor and I were embarking on a quest that was supposed to take us into the depths of our own inner being: a pilgrimage to discover the true meaning of what it is to be human.

Maybe we were crazy, but I don't think so. Even after what happened to Gregor, even after *everything*, I still don't think so.

* * *

At first, of course, it was very difficult down there. Training can't really prepare a person for the experience of living and working in three-times-shipspin gravity. The techs had remodelled our bodies and retuned our biochemistry so that we were physically adapted to local conditions, but they couldn't retune our reflexes and habits; we had to do that ourselves, as we went along. Everyone started off clumsy and stupid, and no matter how hard we'd trained and how hard we tried we *stayed* clumsy and stupid for months. One of the reasons planetdroppers always attack their work-schedule so relentlessly, I guess, is that the only desire their minds can accommodate during the first few months is to get it over with.

Eventually, though, we got used to it all: the legs, the weight, the open spaces, the odours, the weather. It became, quite literally, *second nature* to us. Without even being consciously aware of it, we gradually became comfortable.

After three or four months, all those legendary things I was looking forward to when I first volunteered—sunlit blue skies and windblown rain; oceans and mountains; humanoid aliens, and multitudinous insects, and all the flowers of the forest—gradually became as magical and as fascinating as I'd expected them to be. The hopeful dreams which had turned into nightmares turned back into hopeful dreams again. My alien flesh no longer seemed like a prison; it became an opportunity, a precious instrument of personal destiny.

It was the same for Gregor, maybe more so. There came a day when he said: "It was worth it. It really was worth it. This is *natural* life—the only real life there is. When we go back, we'll look on this as the time we touched the ground, the time we got in touch with what we truly are."

"Yes," I said, "we will." I meant it.

By the time all that began to happen our people had learned half a dozen of the local languages and befriended almost all of the local tribes. The natives had realised by then that we weren't gods or demons, but fairly ordinary folk, with whom they could get drunk and swap tall tales around the campfire. The Quiborians aren't progressives, of course; they weren't hungry to acquire the gadgets we had in order to change their life-styles, and their interest in us was simple curiosity, not so very different from our interest in them. We all got along reasonably well.

The tribes we contacted were mostly plainspeople—like our own ancestors, the intelligent humanoid natives evolved in a subtropical grassland habitat—but some of them had gone back into the fringes of the rainforest, which formed a huge belt across the continent on which we'd landed. The fringe-dwellers regarded the deeper, uninhabited forest as the dark and magical heart of their world, and their collective imagination populated it with all manner of strange beings, natural and supernatural. The tales they told about the interior of the forest were the wildest and weirdest of all the fantasies the Quiborians owned.

I don't know exactly when I decided that my personal mission—the mission which I intended to undertake when the routine work was done—would take me into the heart of the forest. Maybe it was always at the back of my mind. I do know that the first time I mentioned the possibility, obliquely, to Gregor it immediately met up with a reflection and an echo. It was tacitly assumed, from that moment on, that ours was a shared purpose, and we laid our plans together, building desire into ambition with mutual encouragement.

We realised that we'd need help from natives who had some experience of the conditions we'd face, and who knew how to cope with the everyday business of finding food and staying healthy. We didn't anticipate any particular problems—we were immune to all the native viruses because the Quiborian genetic system isn't compatible with DNA—but still we had to be careful. We could eat most of the local produce, because our proteins are built out of the same amino acids as the Quiborians', and most of the simpler chemical constituents of our bodies are identical with theirs, but by the same token we could be poisoned by many of the things that poisoned them. We were also a potential source of food to many of their protozoan and metazoan parasites.

"It's not going to be easy to recruit the kind of help we need," I pointed out to Gregor. "We can't just hire guides and porters, because the natives have no concepts of exploration or employment. We have to find some way of hitching up with indigenes who are interested in going into the interior for their own purposes."

"It can be done," he assured me. "We just have to figure out a way of forming a common cause with the local priest-magicians. It shouldn't be too difficult to arrange a meeting of minds."

He was right. In some ways the Quiborians are very different from humans, but in others they're uncannily similar. They have three sexes, each one of which is 'female' with respect to one of the other two sexes and 'male' with respect to the other, so that their marital arrangements produce triads, multi-triads or open-ended chains rather than mere pairs. In any family the parents are mothers to some of their children and fathers to others. Their sexual organs are associated with their mouths rather than their excretory organs: the tongue doubles as the organ of intromission, their wombs are sacs which lie in front of the cavity which holds their lungs, and the lower jaw is hinged like a python's to facilitate birth. On the other hand, just as their basic physique is determined by the logic of their situation, so are their fundamental ideas and beliefs. They have heads with forward-facing eyes, hands with opposable thumbs and good stout legs; they reason the way we do, and they have magical and religious beliefs much like those of our ancestors. A meeting of minds was infinitely easier to arrange than any kind of intimate intercourse of the flesh.

The Quiborian tribes we contacted were very various in the details of their supernatural beliefs, but they all had specialist wise men of some kind to whom the spiritual welfare of each tribe was entrusted, and all these specialists had to leave their tribes for a while in order that they might be initiated into the particular mysteries of their various creeds. Gregor found out that it was the custom among one of the forest tribes that at a certain critical stage in their training their apprentice wise men had to go deep into the forest, in the company of the older men to whom they were apprenticed, so that the secrets of the ancients might be imparted to them.

As chance would have it, this handing-over of magical responsibility, which only happened rarely—at intervals roughly equal to a fifth of one of our generations—was due at exactly the right time to suit both our official and private agendas.

"The apprentices come back alone," he told me. "They leave the teachers behind. As near as I can translate it, the old men are deemed to have 'joined the company of the elders'. That means, I suppose, that they've gone to a kind of Heaven. They're understandably vague about the details, but it seems to involve both ecstasy and immortality. It's a reward for the service which they've rendered their people, their ancestors, and their gods. The journey into the forest is a solemn and sacred business forbidden to laymen, but I think they might let us tag along; because we're outside their traditional categories we're not subject to their taboos."

Gregor was right about our immunity to their taboos. When he first hinted to the local wise man that we'd be interested the old man didn't throw up his hands in horror. When we asked him right out whether it would be possible for us to accompany his party, his only reservation seemed to be that we'd have to swear not to tell the other tribesmen what we saw. He actually seemed to think that it would be a good thing for the 'starmen with impotent tongues'—that's what they called us, as near as it will translate—to meet the supposedly-immortal elders, so that the elders would have the opportunity to adjust their ancient wisdom to take account of us. I suspect that there was also a little inter-tribal oneupmanship involved, in that our hosts could tell their neighbours for the next few generations that the people who'd come down from the sky had made a point of paying their respects to their ancients in preference to anyone else's idols and fetishes.

* * *

We didn't tell our fellow planetdroppers much about what we were doing; the expedition was thinly spread about the territory by that time, and the others were getting into private projects or fascinations of their own. We just reported that we were going into the interior, and spun a line about collecting data and specimens. The others didn't ask too many questions, probably because most of their lines of enquiry were similarly phoney.

When we finally set off we were a party of six; there was the older-generation magician from whom we'd sought permission, three apprentices, and the two of us. Apparently they always started off with a triad of magicians—one of each sex—but the hazards of life usually reduced the group to two or one by the time the hand-over became due. One of the old magician's original partners had died in an epidemic, the other had been killed in a small war. He confided when we got to know one another a little better that the three youngsters weren't really ready to take over, but said that he had to take them now because it would be a terrible disaster for the tribe if he were to die without having done it.

At that time I had only a sketchy impression of what this particular tribe's religion and its associated magical practices were like. I had grown used to thinking of those sorts of things in generic terms, as data for the re-cords. I knew, though, that they had a particular reverence for flowers, and that they thought of their ultimate ancestors as godlike flowers. That may sound eccentric, but by their standards it was curiously plausible. All the languages of the Quiborian forest tribes have words for "flower" which are closely linked to their words for "mouth"—which makes reasonable sense in terms of their anatomy. A flower contains a plant's reproductive organs just as their mouths contain theirs. Every Quiborian plant has three different kinds of flowers corresponding to the almost-universal trisexual pattern, each with a tongue-like 'stigma' receptive to one kind of 'pollen' which also produces another kind of 'pollen' of its own; each flower, when it ultimately becomes a seed-pod, produces flowers of one of the other kinds.

It was reasonable enough in imaginative terms—however nonsensical it was in evolutionary terms—for unsophisticated forest tribesmen to believe that all extant species, including their own, had been born from some magical plant. Out on the plain, where the grasses were all wind-pollinated and there were very few flowering plants, the natives tended to appoint mythical chimeras as progenitors of themselves and various species to which they were related as hunters or competitors, but in the flower-filled forest the people saw things differently.

Given that our tribesmen thought they were the descendants of a magical flower, it seemed fairly reasonable that they should also credit their hopes of immortality to a flower, so I wasn't unduly surprised or interested to learn that our expedition into the forest was represented by our companions as a journey to the place where a particular kind of magical flower grew. The name of this flower was complicated, being closely associated with the words which the tribesmen used to describe coitus, thus carrying connotations of physical union and orgasmic pleasure as well as the prolongation of life.

"Do you think there really is a flower of some kind?" I asked Gregor, once all this had been explained to us.

"I guess there'll be a real flower of *some kind*," he said, "which native belief invests with all kinds of magical significance and curative potency, but it'll probably be a perfectly ordinary flower of little or no intrinsic worth. You know how these things are." That was when he was being scrupulously realistic, though. He also had moods when he was more entranced with the essential romance of the idea. "Wouldn't it be a coup," he said once, "if we really could bring back the philosopher's stone in the form of an alien flower: a drug which induced a quasi-sexual ecstasy and made men immortal. It's the one real tragedy of our existence that our biotechnologists, for all their metamorphic artistry, have never made much headway in extending the human lifespan."

I was happy enough to play along. "That's two miracles already," I observed, "so you might as well credit the thing with the power to work just as well for humans as it does for its own favourite children. It's a pity that its gifts seem to be reserved for the wisest of wise men, though. Ordinary folk seemingly have to be content to live lives which are nasty, brutish and short—and two out of three wise men evidently perish before being able to claim their reward. If we did take something like that back to the worldship, you can bet your legs that it would be co-opted by the Upper Echelon. The likes of you and I certainly wouldn't get the benefit of it."

"Finding something like that would make us heroes," Gregor said, airily. "We'd be elevated to the Upper Echelon overnight. And why should it be impossible? Do you know how many of the medicines we use aboard the worldship can trace their ancestry back to by-products of the plants of

Old Earth?"

"I know how few can trace their ancestry back to the specimens brought back by ancient teams of planetdroppers," I countered. "Probably less than ten. Alternative genetic systems often throw up useful structural materials, but we're first cousins to the plants of Old Earth, biochemically speaking. *That* may look like a lily, but it's alien through and through."

I was pointing at a nearby bush, whose flowers were indeed like lilies. They were every bit as beautiful by human standards as they were by the standards of the indigenes.

"I wish you could explain that to the stinging and biting insects," Gregor complained. "They seem to find my blood reasonably digestible, and their stings hurt me even more than they hurt our companions."

"A capacity for destruction is far more easily shared than the potential for improvement," I reminded him.

* * *

I could still speak lightly of such things during the first few days of the journey, but as we went deeper into the forest it became increasingly apparent that Gregor had a serious problem. The forest was full of insect life, and many of the insects were bloodsuckers. Although they could draw far more nourishment from the animals which lived in the forest, the breakdown products of human blood were neither entirely useless nor poisonous to them—and in any case, their instincts directed them to attack anything of a suitable size. In adapting us for life on the surface our biotechnicians had given us skins which were not unlike the indigenes' in colour and texture, and the insects attacked us as frequently as they attacked our companions. These bites were no more than a nuisance to me, but it gradually became apparent that they were having a worse effect on Gregor.

At first, Gregor's reaction seemed to be straightforwardly allergic, and it responded well enough to our standard anti-allergy drugs, but that wasn't the end of the matter. He became increasingly prone to fits of fever and to exhaustion. The medicines we carried with us countered the symptoms well enough, but were ineffective against the underlying cause—and so, by slow degrees, Gregor grew weaker.

When I became anxious about him, I tried to find out from our companions how far we still had to go before we reached our destination, and how many days would pass before we returned to the tribal territory, but the natives' arithmetic was very rudimentary. Their counting went one-two-three-few-many, and the difference between 'few' and 'many' depended on the context. At first I assumed that the old man's assurances that we had "a short way" to go and that we would return in "a few" days meant that there was no need to worry, but it transpired that this was one of the contexts in which 'short' and 'few' covered a wider spectrum than usual. Unfortunately, the further we went the more rapidly Gregor's health deteriorated.

I guessed that what had happened was that one of the biting insects had injected into Gregor's bloodstream some local equivalent of the malarial parasite which, although unable to complete its natural lifecycle in his alien cells, was nevertheless capable of obtaining sufficient nutrition from his tissues to multiply. Perhaps it would have been harmless if it hadn't been in an alien environment, and perhaps the toxins it was producing were merely accidental by-products of its unusual diet, but Gregor was certainly suffering, and our medical kit had no means of countering the particular poisons which were harming him.

I asked the wise man if *he* had medicine to cope with Gregor's problem, but all he could come up with was a foul-smelling potion with which to anoint the patient's forehead and stomach, and a ritual dance. The dance was elegant enough—I taped it, dutifully—but it wasn't the slightest help to Gregor.

I called the others and told them we were in trouble, but the expedition had no aircraft of any kind, and such vehicles as we did have were too flimsy to make progress through the forest undergrowth. The advice we received was, as I expected, that we abandoned the journey instantly and set out to retrace our steps.

When I mentioned to the old man that we might go back he flipped his nose—it wasn't a rude gesture, more like our shoulder-shrug—but made it clear that if I decided to do that, Gregor and I would have to make the journey alone. He had a sacred mission of his own to fulfil, and nothing could make him abandon it. I could understand his point of view.

The apprentice magicians were quite willing to help me carry Gregor once he was too ill to walk—indeed, they constructed a litter with remarkable speed and efficiency—but they would only carry him one way: onwards to their own destination.

I had no choice. I knew that I couldn't get him back on my own. I had to hope that his body had the resilience to survive and recover from the poisoning if he did not have to exert himself walking.

Onwards, therefore, we went.

* * *

Even in the midst of my anxieties I couldn't help noticing how very beautiful the forest was.

It wasn't so much the individual flowers, because the range of their shapes and colours and sizes wasn't much different from the flowers I'd grow up with on the worldship, but their sheer riotous *confusion* was something entirely alien to the orderliness of worldship life. Worldship ecology is controlled, entirely under human dominion, but in the Quiborian wilderness things are the other way around. The Quiborians aren't agriculturalists; their management of the ecology is absolutely rudimentary. Their presence and ways of life affect the environment of the fringes and the grasslands, because that's their natural habitat, but in the deep forest they're strangers, moving through a landscape to which they're irrelevant, to whose dominion they must submit.

Gregor and I were in the same situation; we too had to submit to the awful, beautiful dominion of the flowers of the forest.

The air of the forest was rich, warm, damp and full of odours. The trees were ten times the height of a man—even a man with legs. All the trees bore flowers, and the creepers and vines which borrowed their branches for support mingled their own flowers with them, as did the low-lying vegetation which grew in the open spaces where the sunlight filtered through the outer crowns. Even the parasite-plants which grew in the darker coverts and on the huge boles of the older trees put forth little blossoms. And it wasn't just the flowers that were colourful: their pollinators were often just as spectacular. There were brightly-plumaged little birds with fast-fluttering wings, and countless insects whose transparent wings shone iridescent in the dappled light.

Some of the flowers were clever mimics. In the ecosphere which gave us birth it was common for harmless and edible insects to mimic those which had stings or were poisonous, to discourage potential predators, but the Quiborian ecosphere is differently balanced. The Quiborian forest is far richer in insectivorous plants than any Earthly forest, and it's the plants rather than the insects which go in for deceptive mimicry. I found several species of flowering plants which mimicked ones from which the insects could draw nectar, but whose stigmas were adapted as snares, which could entrap visiting insects by coiling around them and then send filaments into their flesh to draw out the nutrients.

We saw very little of the larger animals of the forest, most of which were nocturnal, but there were lemuroid creatures which swung through the canopy, hooting and chattering. We sometimes saw triads of medium-sized herbivores like little deer with coats dappled for camouflage, usually with litters of young in train. Once or twice we saw predators equivalent to Earthly big cats, but they mostly stayed up in the trees by day. At night we sometimes heard them screeching, but they never came close to us. The wise man put it down to the power of his amulets, but I think they just knew better than to attack parties of armed men.

All the apprentices carried bows and arrows, and they were very skilful. They never had to use them defensively, but they frequently shot ground-nesting birds for supper. Gregor and I shared the meals which they made; their meat was quite adequate to human nutritional needs provided that we kept up with the standard dietary supplements. The birds didn't taste very nice, of course, but when you're living rough you soon get used to treating eating as a purely functional matter with no aesthetic component.

It would all have been wonderful, if it hadn't been for the bites and the stings, and Gregor's illness. He did seem to improve a little when he no longer had to walk, but the improvement was temporary. I fed him lots of fluid to protect him from dehydration—there was no shortage of water in the forest and our sterilization kit was a great boon both to ourselves and the natives—but he found it increasingly difficult to keep solid food down and he was losing weight rapidly. To make matters worse, the old man was also beginning to show signs of distress—and he was the only one who knew where we were going.

"Everything is good," he said to me, when I tried to find out what would happen if *he* became too ill to continue. "Soon we meet the ancestors. Soon I am one of them. End of all disease, end of all pain. Everything is good."

I spoke his language reasonably well by then, but the language itself set limits on the sophistication of possible conversation. It simply didn't have the words to frame the questions I really wanted to ask, and the old man couldn't or wouldn't make an extra effort to explain. It was no use trying to quiz the members of the triad; they were looking forward to their initiation into the mysteries, but they didn't have the least idea what to expect.

* * *

By the time we reached our destination the old man was barely coherent, Gregor was barely alive, and I was beginning to suffer myself. It didn't help that we had to climb a long, steep mountain-slope, and then descend into a crater. The climb took a lot out of me, and the old man barely made it.

The crater was presumably volcanic, but the volcano had been cold for millions of years. The air was a lot cooler up there, and the forest was thinner because the ground was much drier—except, I suppose, for the area around the shores of the central lake which I glimpsed from the crater's rim.

Inside the crater, of course, we found the flowers from which the tribesmen thought they were descended, and to whose care they eventually returned their wisest and best. There was no temple and no garden; the things just grew wild wherever their seed happened to fall and find the necessities of life. People like us, I guess, might have tried to gather them together and planted them in groves, but not the Quiborians. The Quiborians let them find their own pattern.

The ancestor-trees were scattered throughout the crater, although they weren't all, in the strict sense, 'ancestor-trees'. The first members of the species I saw weren't among the sacred ones, although I had sufficient imagination to know, as soon I'd seen one, what remained to be seen.

I guess the trees on which the sacred flowers grew were simply the most successful of the many predatory plant-species which lived in the forest—certainly they were the biggest. Maybe their flowers had started out as mimics, like most others of their kind, but had eventually found it more profitable, in terms of the cut-throat marketplace of natural selection, to give up subtlety in favour of brute force.

When they were closed the flowers of the ancestor-trees were fairly unobtrusive, but they were mounted on long, snakelike stalks which could lower them from above with some vigour, and when they opened out—which they could do with remarkable rapidity—they had stigmas which were very long and equally snakelike. These were powerful enough to hold on to most of the animals of the forest, including the deer-like herbivores.

High in the branches of that first ancestor-tree, half-hidden by the discreet foliage, I saw half a dozen species of animals I'd never seen before, plus a deer and a couple of lemuroids. Each one of them must have been hauled up into the crown at some time past for consumption at leisure. A couple of them were little more than husks, and a few bones scattered in the humus beneath the tree suggested that the remains of a couple more had been let fall—but not recently. Most of the tree's captives—I counted eleven, although there may have been one or two small ones invisible in the higher parts of the crown—were still alive.

At first, I couldn't understand why so many of the tree's captives were alive. The set-up made me think initially of web-spinning spiders, which bind their prey tightly and inject a digestive poison which liquefies their insides, ready for drinking. But that was the wrong analogy; the relationship between the trees and *their* prey was more complicated. I realised fairly quickly that the trees were actually *feeding* their captives with a kind of nectar, partly to keep them alive and partly to maintain the production of the blood which their intrusive filaments were leeching away. It was domestication rather than mere murder, like keeping cows for milking.

I'd never noticed the mimic flowers treating their insect prey this way, but that was just a failure of observation. On the way back, in spite of my deteriorating health, I managed to confirm that it was a routine procedure, which the ancestor-trees had carried one step further.

I was immediately able to work out, of course, what the old man had come to find, and what he had come to do. Before I encountered the first of the *real* ancestor-trees I was quite ready for the sight of it.

* * *

Some, at least, of the tribal wise men *were* still alive, and had been preserved by the clever metabolism of the predator-trees for many years longer than they could have lived unaided. They lived in thorny cages of flesh high above the ground, their flesh penetrated by hundreds of vampiric rootlets; but they lived without disease and without discomfort, and retained their ability to think, to dream, and to converse with their neighbours.

Eventually, no doubt, they died like others of their kind, like all the other victims of the trees. While they still lived, though, their lotus-eater existence was not without curiosity or purpose.

Sometimes the elders were only two or three to a tree, but they were usually more crowded. The wise men evidently didn't like to commit themselves to trees without fairly near neighbours, and those who were few within the branches of one captor were always close enough to at least one neighbouring tree to be able to converse with its inhabitants. I suspect, although I can't be sure, that messages could be passed along a line of communication from any part of the strange community to any other.

For some time after I first realised what was going on it seemed slightly absurd. I couldn't quite see the biological sense in it; it simply didn't seem economical for the tree to feed its prey at the same time as it fed *off* its prey. We nourish our fields and our tissue-cultures very carefully indeed, so that we may dine all the more sumptuously upon their produce—agriculture and animal husbandry gave our ancestors the first of their two great leaps forward, turned them into progressives, and set their feet on the road to the stars—but we don't feed them with the produce of our own bodies; that would be sending the nutrients round in a futile circle.

In time, though, I began to see the sense in it. I explained it all to Gregor as best I could, while he was still in a state to listen.

"The ancestor-trees *do* consume their captives, little by little," I told him. "They discard what's left when they're all used up. But they work at a tree's pace, in the context of a tree's lifetime. I don't know how old these particular trees are, but I suspect they outlive the tribesmen by a factor of two or three hundred. It makes perfect sense for them to *eke out* what is, after all, only one of two sources of nutrition—they have photosynthetic leaves too, of course. The energy-economics might be eccentric, but there *is* profit in suckling their captives on a kind of nectar which keeps them alive and disease-free, so that they can supply the tree with all kinds of nutrients which it can't make for itself. I'd call it symbiosis except that none of the captive animals except the tribesmen gets any advantage out of it. It evolved as parasitism pure and simple—but in the case of the sentient humanoids, there's a kind of payoff in being parasitized. It's not so much *longer* life as *more leisured* life: the acquisition of time that's useless for anything except thinking, but certainly isn't to be despised by thinking beings."

Now we were no longer on the move any more he rallied a little, and he was able to take a keen interest in the trees.

"There's a certain irony in the fact," he mused, appreciatively, "that while the humanoid Quiborians haven't yet developed agriculture and animal husbandry—and perhaps never will—the ingenious flowers of the Quiborian forest have taken advantage of a freak of natural selection to domesticate *them*."

The trees seemed to look after their captives pretty well. The nectar was obviously a more-than-useful food, and the stigmas and stalks which wrapped around the captured animals were mounted with huge blood-red thorns, protecting the prisoners from raids by animal predators and scavengers.

"It would all be different, of course," I said to Gregor, "if the tribesmen were progressives like us. They'd soon have started thinking about the nectar as a crop and as a product. Then they'd have started cultivating the trees, feeding them on animals, selecting for higher yields, ruthlessly exploiting the life-extending panacea for all it was worth . . . all that kind of thing. But the tribesmen aren't progressives; they accept nature as they find it, and offer themselves *to* it instead of breaking and bending it to their will. Hence the elders: willing human sacrifices, preserved by man and tree alike with care and reverence."

Our discussions regarding the trees were all like that to begin with: general, impersonal, and seemingly indifferent. But we both knew well enough what we were doing, and why we couldn't possibly be authentically indifferent.

The tribesmen's mythology was exaggerated, of course: the clever flowers of the magical trees didn't confer immortality, and the euphoria they gifted to their victims probably wasn't "ecstatic", although I can't honestly claim to know *what* might constitute ecstasy for three-sexed Quiborians whose tongues doubled as sex-organs. As tribal idols go, though, the magical god-flower had a lot to offer its worshippers—far more than any of the idols *our* ancestors chose to worship.

* * *

The trees consumed their captives by slow degrees. Their heads and torsos remained longest unaffected, but their limbs atrophied soon after capture, and were gradually reabsorbed into their bodies. The pattern of this induced metamorphosis was presumably connected with the fact that prisoners without limbs were easier by far to hold, and that continuing life depended on the maintenance of the brain. From the viewpoint of the intelligent captives, however, it was a uniquely convenient system, maintaining the mind while slowly diminishing the distractions of the flesh. Because of this preferential wasting of the limbs, most of the ancestors hanging in the trees were virtually legless. Gregor and I were inevitably reminded of our own bodies: the "normal" bodies which we had temporarily abandoned in adapting ourselves for planetary life.

I had no wish to intrude upon the business which the old man and his apprentices had with the elders of their tribe, and while they went about their business I sat apart with Gregor, explaining the last elements of the mysteries into which I had been so unexpectedly initiated.

"They're really very beautiful, Gregor," I told him. "Horrible, certainly, but so awesomely *majestic* in their aspect that even the horror of it becomes beauty of a kind. There's nothing else like them in our known universe—unless something lurks unread and unremembered in the dry, dead records of past planetfalls."

"I don't need persuading," he answered, faintly. "I understand the situation." He knew perfectly well that he couldn't make the return journey. He knew that the choice before him was absurdly simple, and that there was nothing to be said for death, by comparison with an experience no other human had ever had before. He knew that he had already missed the ship, and that the only journey left for him to undertake was a far stranger voyage than ours, into the alien unknown.

There were only two questions to be settled, and both were to do with the problem of loneliness. I didn't have to go in search of the old man to put the first of them to him; he came to me, in spite of the fact that he was hardly able to walk. He *was* a wise man, at least by Quiborian standards, and a kind man too.

"Your friend is not one of us," he said—although he had to use a word for 'marital partner' because his language had no other equivalent for 'friend'. "He is not a child of the flower." They were statements of fact, not refusals. I wasn't disheartened by his words.

"He is not a child of the flower," I agreed. There was no way I could tell him that in a strictly literal sense, *his* people were not descended from this or any flower, but from the forest lemuroids.

"But he is not of the tribes of the grassland, which have forgotten the flower," said the old man, judiciously, "and he is a wise man, of sorts."

"He has much wisdom in his head," I agreed. "Your ancestors might learn from him. Let my friend join your elders, and live among them, in the heart of their small tribe, so that he might share his wisdom with theirs. Let the elders accept him as one of themselves, as one of their company."

It was the longest and most difficult speech I had ever made in that alien language. I hope it was the best.

"He is a starman with an impotent tongue," the old man confirmed, "but he is not a grasslander. There is something in him of . . ."

The last concept was too complex to be easily translatable. The word was the equivalent of 'human being', but it was also related to the words for 'flower' and 'mouth' and 'three-ness'.

"I have spoken to the ancestors," the magician went on. "I too am numbered only one instead of three, but they will take me into a company and your friend also."

The word I've rendered 'company' also had a lot of 'three-ness' about it, and a status inflection. I suppose that to them it wasn't unlike an offer of in-stant promotion from vent-end dirty-hander to Upper Echelon infotech. In fact, 'not unlike' may be ungenerous.

"What about me?" I asked—which was, of course, the second relevant question. "Could I stay too, if I wanted to?"

Gregor, I know, would not have approved of my asking. "Don't be a fool," he would have said. "You may not be a hundred per cent fit, but you can still make the ship. You still have a *real* life to lead. Don't even think about staying." He'd have said it no matter how desperate *he* was for me to stay, no matter how lonely *he* feared to become. I honestly don't know what I'd have done, if it had just been a matter for the two of us to deter-mine. But the old man had a firm opinion.

"You, he and I are *not* three," he said, meaning not a *triad*. "He has no strength left; you are strong enough. You must help the young ones. They are not ready. They are better, if you are with them."

It was a great compliment, in its way. And I knew that Gregor wouldn't be alone: he'd have half a dozen living individuals close at hand, and many other neighbours just a shout away.

"Look after him," I said to the old man—or tried to say, although he clucked a little to tell me that I wasn't making sense, presumably because his language had no word for 'looking after' that was not connected with parenthood and childcare.

"The stars are flowers," he told me, earnestly. In his world-view, of course, they were. "Although his tongue is impotent, we are of the same starborn company."

"That is the truth," I said.

* * *

I wasn't lying when I agreed with the old man. We're all the children of ancient supernovae. The elements which make up our bodies were seeds born from the mouths of primal fire. We're *all* of the same starborn company, in flesh, in body and in mind. I really believe that; and that's why I don't feel bad about what I had to do.

I can't tell you exactly how I felt when we gave them both to the ancestor-tree. The flower took them very gently, and didn't try to make a grab for anyone else. The young magicians dressed all six of us with pretty blooms, and we sang and danced for an hour. I didn't know the words or the steps, but I improvised as best I could, until I was too sick and tired to caper about any longer.

The elders sang with us: all of them. Their voices filled the forest, and echoed from the rocky walls that dressed the crater's rim.

Gregor was very quiet afterwards; when the triad took me away he was better able to speak, and he was at peace. He was feeling no pain—I'm sure of that.

"Goodbye," he called after me. "Good luck. Say hello to the void for me."

"I will," I promised. I wept a little, but only for the pain of separation, not out of grief.

He wasn't dead, after all. He wasn't even lost.

There was no absolute guarantee that it would work, of course, but at least the tree hadn't spat him out immediately, and I figured that if the local biting insects could nourish themselves on his blood, so could the tree. I also told myself that whatever happened, he was certainly no worse off up there in the branches than he would have been buried in the shallow tropical soil. It was all true.

I can't make any guess as to how long he might survive, if he's still alive. The old man and the elders had no way of giving me a clue, given their rudimentary counting system. But that's one of the things Gregor may be able to teach them, if things work out. I'm pretty sure that some of the elders had lived three or four times of their own natural lifespans as guests of the trees. That's enough to learn arithmetic, and a lot besides. In time, perhaps, Gregor might be able to teach them chemistry, physics, cosmology—anything their own thinking can grow to embrace. I don't say that he's a certainty to convert the tribesmen to the cause of progress, but I think there's every chance that he'll give them the opportunity to become progressives if that's what they decide they want to be. If the Quiborians ever get around to building worldships, there's a good chance that the flower which gave birth to the chain of events will be the flower that made Gregor captive, and nourished him for the duration of his second life.

That's a better destiny, in its way, than I'll ever find, out here in the comfortable void. He'll have to pay the price in good red blood, and he'll have to hope that the sacrifice is acceptable, but if it is he might outlive us all. If he does, he has the chance to add his wisdom—*our* wisdom—to the traditional lore of one of Quibor's tribes. Gregor isn't a man any longer; he's an *elder* now. Impotent mouth or not, he has a chance to make a difference to the history and the destiny of the people who befriended us. Maybe they won't listen, and maybe they won't understand, but there's just a chance that we planted a seed that will grow.

Maybe there'll be even more to it than the creation of one more set of humanoid progressives *en route* to worldships and the freedom of the limitless dark—because what we found on that mountain is something which is, as far as we know, absolutely unprecedented. A *plant* formed by the forces of natural selection to be a farmer of animals, including sentient animals. I left Gregor to be the fruit of a tree which already had eight humanoid captives, and when I think about that entity as a whole, rather than simply as the sum of its parts, I can see unique evolutionary potential in it. It's a new kind of association of species: a tree which has acquired brains. In time . . . who knows what the evolutionary future of that compound being might be?

The Quiborian wise men saw the unique potential in that association; they knew when they discovered the ancestor-tree what superhuman implications it had. They're wrong about its role in their own origins, and about most of its supposed magical powers, but they're right to see it as a remarkable gift of nature, as an opportunity for they and their descendants to be and to become something very different and something much finer than the people of the grasslands. They may be primitives, but they're not fools. They taught me a great deal, about the universe we live in and about our place in it; they taught me that there's more than one way to be rid of useless legs, and that ours isn't the one and only way forward. Gregor got a chance to be part of that, and I can honestly say that I envy him, at least a little. I dare say that it was he, not I, who came out of our adventure best.

Not many would agree with me, of course. Most will doubtless side with the medics. They'll look at me and think: "He's a monster! He's a madman, crazy enough to grow legs! How can we take seriously anything he says?" I am a monster; that's undeniable. I did grow legs, so that I might go down to the bottom of a deep, dire well, far away from the comforting darkness of the space between the stars. But I tell you this: *I have touched the ground, and I have looked into my soul and found the roots of my being . . . and you, who are faithful children of the friendly void, have not.*

LAYERS OF MEANING

There are, it is said, visionary moments of intense experience which can carry us beyond the fragile sliver of the present into the greater reaches of time, when we can grasp the context which gives meaning to the apparently trivial incidents of everyday life. Proust experienced such a moment when the taste of the *madeleine* dipped in tea recalled in him not merely the memory but the whole texture and significance of childhood. This is the story of a similar moment when a young curate, in the act of slicing the top from a boiled egg, was thrown by the merest whiff of hydrogen sulphide into an experience which, though it occupied only a fraction of a second in itself, linked past and future into a vast panorama.

The odour of hydrogen sulphide is not pleasant, but it *is* powerful, and thus can easily constitute a trigger, releasing memories associated with it in the distant past which have long lain dormant. It is not renowned as a hallucinogen, but there may be resources locked up in the human mind which themselves need only an appropriate trigger, and the explosive release of pent up memories might conceivably, in this case at least, have acted like a detonator priming a more devastating mental event. Whether this event was the product of the curate's imagination, or some amazing inflow of divine truth, there is no way we can know. However we choose to regard it, though, we must surely take the curate's revelation seriously, for there is no doubt that insights do visit holy men in the most mysterious ways.

* * *

The first impression summoned to the curate's mind was certainly a memory, of days gone by when his family kept a flock of chickens and the first duty ever to give his youthful existence a purpose was to collect the eggs which they laid. This was not usually a difficult task, but was not unskilful, for the chickens had the run of a big wooden barn, and were sometimes inclined to lay in secret places.

It was as if they were consciously engaged in a game with him, by which their task was to conserve their eggs for the making of hatchlings instead of surrendering them to the breakfast table. They rarely succeeded in this, because the curate as a boy had been too clever, and the broody chickens would often unwittingly lead him to the prize; when eggs were lost it was almost invariably because their layers abandoned them, so that they went rotten, and when broken produced that unmistakable unpleasant stench.

No sooner had the curate caught the image of himself in the barn, though, than the barn began to change, and he saw another boy, who was not himself but perhaps a son or grandson in some future time, wandering an aisle between great banks of tiny cages, where literally thousands of hens were penned, with food delivered to them by plastic tubes and their eggs conveyed away by helter-skelter chutes. There was no labour now for the boy to do save check that all was well, and while he watched the scene continued to shift, so that the degree of automation of the system increased. Outside the barn, he knew, a forest of electric cables slowly extended to connect the apparatus within to control mechanisms without: green screens where words and figures marched aloft in militaristic orderliness.

Soon, the hens began to change too. The curate knew nothing of electronics, and could understand only vaguely what was happening to the regulatory mechanisms of the factory farm, but he did know a little of Charles Darwin's theory of evolution, and was able to grasp the basic idea of genetic engineering even though he knew nothing of DNA and the techniques by which it would one day be manipulated. He understood that scientists had learned how to interfere with the "blueprints" which eggs contained in order to grow into hens, and could thus remake the hens in subtle ways, to make them better layers. From his viewpoint in the aisle the curate (seeming to move now from one descendant *persona* to another with thoughtless ease) watched the hens become fatter, watched their heads disappear so that the tubes conveying food went directly into their bodies, and watched the production of eggs become faster and faster.

These curious headless, wingless, legless hens grew bigger and bigger, losing even their feather coats, until they were nothing but great white mounds of flesh, as big as elephants, churning out eggs with incredible speed.

At this point the curate—or perhaps one of the others whose consciousness he seemed to be sharing in series—remembered a kind of sermon which had been preached to him.

"Think," someone had said, "not of an egg as a hen's way of making another hen; think rather of a hen as an egg's way of making another egg. Everything that the hen is to be is written in the molecules of the egg, and a hen is only one being which might be inscribed there. All birds, all animals, even human beings, grow from eggs into which their identities are written by the hand of God, and all the beings in Creation are merely ways by which eggs make more eggs.

"If the nature of God is to be judged by the contemplation of nature—if we and other of His creations are deemed to be made in His image—then we might easily conceive of God as the Cosmic Egg, and of the moment when His universe was set in motion as the moment when that Egg began to develop. If this be so, then there is nothing ungodly in the belief that all life in the universe has evolved from common ancestry, for there is nothing in the developing pattern of evolution but the unfolding of a plan by which primordial eggs devise better and better ways of making more eggs.

"Human beings may be nothing more than the eggs' first attempts to reach a knowledge of the nature of their Creation, and by that means, a knowledge of their Creator. If we realise this, it will teach us a true humility, because it will become clear to us that there may in future be other beings better adapted by their eggs to this purpose, compared to whom we might be but the first feeble experiments."

The curate now found that his vantage point was no longer confined to the egg-farm; his vision expanded to take in the work that was being done to eggs in order to make them grow into these strange forms, which could produce more eggs in such abundance. He became aware that it was not simply the eggs of birds that were being altered, but the eggs of fish, the eggs of silkworms, the eggs of oysters, the eggs of frogs, and even eggs stripped from the wombs of sheep and cattle.

Eventually the information encoded in eggs taken from the ovaries of human beings also began to be rewritten by these ambitious creators. These reworkings of genetic blueprints grew so ambitious, as time extended into the curate's far future, that it ceased to matter where an egg had come from, for many that were used had not come from natural organisms at all, but from other laboratory-created entities whose appointed function it was to produce various multitudes of eggs.

The curate saw eggs designed to produce foodstuffs, and eggs designed to produce materials used in building, in the manufacture of machines, and ever and always eggs for the production of more eggs. He realised, remembering the sermon he had heard, that this was simply part and parcel of the expanding pattern of evolution and Creation; and that genetic engineers were simply one more way devised by eggs for the production of more and more eggs, which would in their turn produce eggs more abundantly and more cleverly than they had ever been produced before.

As the story that had somehow been pregnant in his own ill-fated breakfast egg went on, reaching further and further into the future, he saw eggs produced which were designed to be eaten alive, to grow within the bodies of human beings as symbiotes which would gradually devour the flesh of the body, merging with it and replacing the organs which nature had provided with more efficient ones. He watched humans, under the influence of such eggs, transformed like Achilles' ship, part by part, until nothing remained of them that had been blueprinted into their own original eggs; even their brains had been consumed and regenerated, without interruption to the continuity of their inhabiting personalities.

These eggs, the curate saw, were rebuilding the fleshly envelopes of human souls, remoulding them into finer clay. The beings which emerged from such metamorphoses were stronger, much longer-lived, immune to all disease. At first, they seemed still to be men, more perfect but essentially unaltered, but the processes of self-change which men had instituted did not stop there.

He saw men adapted for shapeshifting, so that they could alter themselves fluidly, like werewolves of old but in controlled and much more various fashion. He saw men adapted in their limbs so that their organic nerves could be interfaced with the electronic wires of machines, so that men could blend themselves with their instruments: their vehicles, their factories, their artificial intelligences. He saw men adapted so that they could link their nervous systems one to another, to fuse their being with one another in many different ways. And all this was controlled and managed by the living eggs on which they feasted.

There came to his mind now more sermons, which he or the others with whom he was in tune might one day hear, though they took a crazy form in which the play with genes was reflected in play with words. He had heard of a philosopher named Nietzsche, who had promised the world of the future übermensch, and he heard now that the promise had come true, and that the world had passed into the charge of overmen, who were also ova-men; that the world he lived in was ova-thrown and ova-taken, and a new one ova-grown and ova-wrought, governed more by ova-seers than ova-lords, and that all of this was but part of the great ova-flow which had been instituted in the moment of Creation and which must proceed until a kind of great circle was complete and the souls of men, reunited into the single great soul of *all mankind*, would become what they or it had in reality always been: the intelligence of God, the ultimate JEH-OVA-H; the Cosmic Egg which was all the eggs that there ever had been or that ever would be.

In the climax of this vision, which had been reached with an almighty rush that hardly gave the visionary time to wonder what on Earth had possessed him, the point of view which had in the beginning been contained within a single small boy, and had unfolded through the myriad minds of that boy's descendants, exploded into a galaxy of points of consciousness which were one as well as many: a sidereal system of souls infinite in extent. In spite of this, the sensation was as sharp as the initial sensation of memory; it seemed to the curate just as real, just as compelling, just as powerful and as urgent as any sensation ever could be or ever would be, as long as he might live.

* * *

"My dear fellow," said the bishop, his host—the voice dispelling utterly by its awful mundanity the vision which had momentarily occupied his mind—"I fear that your egg is bad."

"Oh no, my lord," said the curate, anxious politeness compelling his reply. "Indeed it is quite good—in parts."

THE OEDIPUS EFFECT

As Simon Sweetland locked the doors of his dilapidated Mini he looked up, as was his habit, to survey the graffiti sprayed on the windowless wall of concrete which was the northern face of DPR Coventry. It was, as ever, a disappointing sight; the Midland school of street art was still in its super-naïve phase.

Ignoring the obscenities and the Rorschach-blot squiggles he squinted through his spectacles at the one item which had seemed to hold a possibility of better things to come. Originally it had read: YOU DON'T HAVE TO BE WEIRD TO WORK HERE BUT IT HELPS—an unoriginal sentiment, remarkable in context only because the word "weird" was correctly spelled. Then someone had crossed out WEIRD and substituted TALENTED—a predictable defensive ploy only slightly dignified by the fact that the words had been psychokinetically embossed, obviously not by any of the local Temps but by some passing hotshot from the Metropolis. Then the original artist had crossed out TALENTED and substituted FREAKY. Simon had been hoping to see a fourth move for three weeks now, but Talent and literary flair somehow never seemed to go together.

He was not tempted to make any contribution of his own; he was essentially one of the DPR's—and life's—spectators. Not only was he devoid of psychokinetic Talent but of any other noticeable power to impose his personality upon the environment. Weird and freaky he might be, but superhuman he was not; he was a mere theorist, one of the fortunate few dozen which the scientific civil service felt it worthwhile to devote to the study of Talents, with a view to one day discovering an explanation for their existence.

He crossed the almost-empty car park—he was, as was his habit, twenty minutes early—and entered the building. He passed through the empty lobby and went upstairs to his office, where he hung up his coat before taking up his station behind his desk. Then he unfolded his copy of *The Guardian* and began to read.

His telephone rang and he picked it up, despite the fact that it was not yet nine o'clock. "Someone to see you—a Mr. Fay," said Marcia, in an aggrieved tone. Simon inferred that she had only just arrived, and he knew full well that she did not like to have work thrust at her even before the day had officially begun. He had never heard of any Mr. Fay.

"Send him up," he said, wearily, closing *The Guardian* but not bothering to hide it.

Two minutes later there was a knock on his door. A young man in a smart suit came in, a practised smile appearing upon his well-scrubbed features, as if at the flick of some mysterious internal switch.

"Dr. Sweetland?" he said, with careful enthusiasm. "I'm Lewis Fay, of Family Provident."

Simon's heart sank. "I'm quite well insured, thank you," he said, reflexively. "I don't need any financial advice whatsoever."

The smile neither cracked nor quivered. "I'm not a salesman, Dr. Sweetland. I'm Senior Claims Adjuster, Midlands and West. I'd like to talk to you about your paper in the current issue of the *Journal of Paranormal Studies*, if I may."

Simon's eyebrows lifted in astonishment. He had not realised that anyone outside the DPR and a few university departments ever read the *JPS*. He had been a regular contributor for more than ten years—promotion in the scientific civil service was rumoured to be heavily dependent on one's publication record—but no one had ever before shown the slightest interest in any of his papers. In fact, Simon rarely bothered to read the journal himself, though he dutifully placed the quarterly issues on the bookshelf behind his desk when they arrived (usually six to eight weeks late). He took it for granted that all the other papers, as well as his own, were produced under the spur of career-building necessity, and that they would either be routine exercises in number-crunching or flights of philosophical fancy devoid of any semblance of empirical support.

"You mean," he said, warily wondering whether Mr. Fay might have the wrong man, "*A New Interpretation of the Precognitive Paradox.*"

"That's the one," said Fay, breezily. "Brilliant work, Dr. Sweetland—I was very impressed. So impressed that I'd like to talk to you about some consultancy work. DPR scientists are allowed to take on outside consultancy work, aren't they?"

Simon's eyebrows were incapable of further elevation, and he was too self-conscious to allow his jaw to drop, so he simply nodded, dumbly. He had, of course, heard rumours of fat retainers paid to senior DPR scientists by companies in return for mysterious advice—usually, he supposed, for covert assistance in identifying and luring away the DPR's more useful Temps—but he had never expected to catch a glimpse of that kind of Gravy Train himself. He was a Head of Department, but he only had one assistant, and was only one step removed from being a mere tester. "Please take a seat," he said, cautiously.

While Lewis Fay lowered himself into the PVC-clad chair which was usually occupied by mothers of that rare but avid breed who would try desperately to convince him that their unprepossessing children had hitherto-unimagined paranormal potential, Simon leaned forward, covering his newspaper with his elbows, and said: "How, exactly, may I help you, Mr. Fay?"

"We would like to retain your services as a consultant," Fay repeated. "The work wouldn't be very time-consuming; it would consist of writing the occasional report, and perhaps appearing in court once now and again as an expert witness. The details are negotiable, but I ought to warn you that the remuneration would be modest, at first. We envisage a fixed retainer in the region of a thousand a year, but there would be a bonus scheme, by which you would get a fee for every successfully-aborted claim of one per cent of the averted payout. It doesn't sound much, I know, but you'll be surprised how it mounts up. In five years time, if you can back up the claims made in your paper, you might be pulling in tens of thousands a year."

Simon clung on to the last vestiges of his composure, and managed to nod as if he received such offers regularly.

"As you've undoubtedly noticed," Fay added, serenely, "recent circumstances have thrown up an excellent test case for your thesis. If you can persuade a jury that what you say in your paper is true, or even that it's possible, it will create such an important precedent that the rest of your career should be plain sailing."

Simon tried valiantly to figure out what Fay was talking about, but he couldn't do it. He felt like a non-swimmer dropped in at the deep end; the circumstances were simply not conducive to orderly and patient mental procedure.

"I'm sorry," he murmured, "but I don't quite see . . . "

Fay beamed—not, this time, the practised smile of welcome and reassurance, but a shark-like grin of casual superiority. Simon had seen similar expressions on the faces of Talented people, and had never liked them. They were expressions which said: "I'm better than you, and I know things you don't, and because of that I can make you do what I want you to."

"I do apologise, Dr. Sweetland," said Lewis Fay, insincerely. "I'm going too quickly, aren't I? One sometimes forgets that academics like yourself, preoccupied with matters of abstract theory, don't always see the practical applications of their work. Far be it from me to try to explain your own ideas to you, but perhaps you wouldn't mind if I run over them for my own benefit, so that I can make sure I'm not making a fool of myself. Then, perhaps, I can, ah, show you where I'm coming from."

Supercilious bastard! thought Simon. But he said nothing, contenting himself with a nod.

"Your paper," said Mr. Fay, calmly, "is about the so-called paradox of precognition, is it not? This arises from the fact that among Paranorms there is a small sub-group who seem to be able, in various slightly different ways, to have foreknowledge of the future, and to be able to issue true prophecies. The paradox, if I understand the matter correctly, comes in when the prophecies are made, and arises because of the effect that the making of a prophecy has on the likelihood of the event in question occurring. I believe you call it the Oedipus effect."

Simon nodded again, and—feeling that he had made enough of a fool of himself already—quickly took up the argument: "That's right. It's so-called because the prophecy that Oedipus would one day kill his father caused his father to set in train the chain of cause-and-effect which later enabled the event to occur. It's not a very good name really, because it refers to a self-fulfilling prophecy, while the effect is usually the other way around; prophecies are more often self-negating than self-fulfilling. If a precog tells you that you're going to die in a plane crash you simply don't take the plane—the fact that the prophecy has been issued prevents it from coming true. That's the paradox."

Fay was still beaming. "And it casts doubt, therefore, on the status of so-called precognitive Talents. If the event which the precognitive foresees doesn't happen because the people forewarned take steps to avert it, how can we claim that he really is seeing the future? Now, as I understand it, the orthodox answer is that the future isn't fixed, and that precognitives can only see *possible* futures. But your paper proposes a different interpretation, doesn't it?"

"It points out that another interpretation is theoretically possible," Simon said, warily. "You see, there are a lot of Talents which aren't under conscious control—paranormal abilities which can't just be summoned up at will, but break out in moments of extreme stress. Talents of that kind are more like emotions than instruments of the will—they're not really things which the paranorms consciously *do*. That's one of the reasons why there are so few really powerful and effective paranorms, and so many who are . . . well, unreliable. What my paper suggests is that some paranorms whose Talents are classified by testers as precognitive are really powerful but undisciplined psychokinetics. The events which they seem to foresee are, in fact, events which they subconsciously intend to *cause*. When they predict that a fly on the window will shortly drop dead in mid-flight they're really anticipating an action which their own psychokinetically-talented subconscious mind will carry out—their foreknowledge may be no more paranormal than my foreknowledge when I say that I'm going to get a rolled-up newspaper and swat the fly."

"Precisely," said Lewis Fay. "A very clever idea, if I may say so."

"It's only speculation," said Simon, "and I don't quite see . . . " Then he stopped, because all of a sudden he *did* see why Family Provident might be interested in his paper. He cursed himself for not having seen it before. After a moment's pause, while he and Mr. Fay watched one another carefully, he said: "You mentioned a test case."

"That's right," said Fay, cheerfully. "Did you see the evening paper last night?"

""No," Simon admitted. "I usually pick one up on the way home, but it was raining, and I couldn't be bothered getting out of the car."

"Of course," said Lewis Fay, as though it were obvious. "And I see that you take *The Guardian*, so you would also have missed the item in this morning's tabloids. There was a death on a building-site in the city centre yesterday. A crane was moving a concrete pile. The chains broke and the pile fell. Nobody was underneath it, but the toppling pile smashed a stack of tiles and sent the shards hurtling in all directions. One of them struck the head of an architect named Thomas Hemdean. It fractured his skull and caused a haemorrhage. He was dead on arrival at the hospital."

"And who predicted it?" asked Simon, his voice hardly above a whisper.

"Nicholas Hemdean—the man's eight-year-old son. He begged his father not to go to work, apparently having described exactly what would happen, in front of four witnesses: his mother, his twelve-year-old sister, a neighbour and the neighbour's twelve-year-old daughter. It was in the local paper last night, and some of the tabloids picked it up for this morning's editions. Apparently the boy had been tested by the DPR at his mother's request, but the evidence for his Talent was considered inadequate. One or two of the papers have suggested that the Department's failure to identify the Talent might have caused the father to disbelieve the prediction—and thus, indirectly, have contributed to his death, but I don't know how far they'll be prepared to take that line of argument. Anyway, you and I know how it really happened, don't we?"

Simon felt suddenly rather sick. "Your company insured this man's life?" he said.

"That's correct," agreed Mr. Fay.

"And you stand to pay out a lot of money if the death was accidental—because of double indemnity?"

"Right."

"But like all insurance companies, you have an exclusion clause in your policies which means that you don't have to pay out at all if someone dies as a result of assignable paranormal action. It then becomes the task of the beneficiary to sue the person responsible for the amount which the policy would have realised."

"It's a necessary precaution, given the kind of world we live in," said Fay, spreading his arms wide. "And the matter of intention is, of course, irrelevant to the matter of responsibility."

Simon could now see the whole pattern, in all its horrific detail. "You want me to write a report," he said, haltingly, "and, if necessary, to give evidence in court, to say that this man's death was caused, unconsciously, *by his own son.*"

"You don't have to prove it," said Fay, agreeably. "You only have to establish that it's *possible*. We don't necessarily expect to get off scot free—we'd be quite happy to settle for a compromise. And you'll get a percentage of any money you save us. At the moment we stand to pay out a hundred and twenty K. We think there's a good chance you can at least save us from the double indemnity. You might also save your department—perhaps yourself, if you were the one who tested the boy—from some bad publicity."

One per cent of sixty thousand pounds, Simon knew, was six hundred pounds—not much more than a fortnight's wages. But Fay had already pointed out that one case would create a vital precedent. The price that was being put on Simon's soul was by no means meagre. How many deaths, he wondered, were predicted by precogs? How many more were claimed to have been predicted by liars and lucky guessers? How many cases a year could Family Provident call into question? Hundreds? Thousands?

"But it's his *eight-year-old son*," said Simon, weakly. "You want me to put the blame for this man's death on his own child."

"On the child's *unconscious desires*," Fay was quick to stress. "Well-documented desires, at that. Didn't Freud say that all boys are unconsciously jealous of their fathers, because they see them as rivals for their mothers' love? Didn't he call *that* effect after Oedipus, too? Quite appropriate really, don't you think?"

Simon simply stared at his visitor, rendered speechless by the nauseous enormity of it all. Lewis Fay stood up, and placed a business card on the desk. "That's my number," he said. "Think it over and give me a ring. I understand your reservations, of course, and only you can decide where your own and your Department's interests lie. I'll be in all day should you wish to contact me. Please don't bother to get up—I can find my own way out."

Even as Lewis Fay turned to go to the door, Simon's telephone began to ring. He picked it up. "There's a call for you," said Marcia, in a breathlessly respectful tone which he had never heard her use before, even when talking to the Division Head. "It's a man from the Sun. Shall I put him through?" She could hardly have sounded more surprised had it been a man from the sun.

"No," said Simon, quickly. "I can't talk to reporters now. Tell him that I'm tied up. And that goes for Carol too. If they keep trying, tell them we'll be available for comment later."

Considering that her remarkable propensity for saying no to callers was the nearest thing to a Talent Marcia had, she sounded surprisingly resentful when she said: "Oh, very well then."

Simon left the phone off the hook, just in case.

* * *

Simon tried to call up the record of Nicholas Hemdean's testing on the computer, but the system was down and he had to go instead to the huge filing cabinet where the scoring-cards were kept. Here he discovered that Nicholas Hemdean had been tested five months earlier by Carol Cloxeter, his one and only assistant.

That made him feel slightly better—not because it might enable him to pass the buck if the Department were to come under fire, but because it explained why he had no memory of the case.

The handwritten notes on the card registered Nicholas as an alleged Dreamer—not only the commonest kind of precog but also the easiest to misidentify—and observed that most of the supposed evidence for the child's talent was not only anecdotal but retrospective; which was to say that the child had mostly claimed to have foreseen the relevant events after they had happened. Tests with Zener cards and dice had given scores no better than average, and the child had been unable to issue any sufficiently-specific predictions to warrant further investigation. Simon knew that there must be several hundred more-or-less identical cards in the file.

He carried the card to Carol's office and showed it to her.

"Can you remember this boy?" he asked.

She looked at the card, furrowing her brow in concentration. Then she looked up and nodded. She had lovely grey eyes, perfectly set off by her large-lensed spectacles, and a very sweet smile. Simon had been half in love with her for two years; unfortunately, she was happily married to one Edward Cloxeter, Consultant Ergonomicist.

"Vaguely," she said. "Very shy boy. Handsome mother, distinctly upmarket—not the usual type at all."

The mothers most ardently desirous of discovering Talent in their offspring tended to be dissatisfied members of the working class. Middle-class parents usually preferred their kids to be normal—by which they meant polite, articulate and high-achieving.

"Why did she bring him in at all?" asked Simon, guardedly.

Carol shrugged. "If he'd had a toothache she'd have taken him to the dentists, and would have been equally relieved to be told that he didn't need a filling. She just wanted professional reassurance that there was nothing to worry about. Why? Has something happened?"

"You didn't see the evening paper?"

"No. We do take it but it's Eddie's really."

Simon sighed. It didn't take a genius to work out what had happened. Mrs. Hemdean had taken Little Nicholas home and told her husband that there was nothing to worry about, and that the boy's dreams would go away in time if they ignored them—like an imaginary playmate or acne. The father had probably been glad to go to work after the child begged him not to, just to prove once and for all that the dreams were nothing to be afraid of. He told Carol what had happened to Thomas Hemdean, but left Lewis Fay out of it for the time being.

"We'd better get the papers and see how much of a problem we have," he said. "Then we'd better go see Mrs. Hemdean and find out what really happened."

"Am I in trouble?" asked Carol, anxiously.

"Of course not," said Simon, wishing that he sounded more convincing. "You did everything right. The papers will probably drop it. They enjoy putting the boot into the DPR, but this isn't in the same league as a juicy story about some wacky Temp fouling things up."

"Yes, of course," she said, though her anxiety was obviously unquieted. "I'll get my coat."

* * *

Simon drove to a local newsagents, where he managed to buy a copy of the previous evening's paper as well as the morning tabloids. The evening paper's coverage was headlined LOCAL ARCHITECT KILLED IN FREAK ACCIDENT, and it presented a relatively sober account of the facts beneath a photograph of the dead man; it only mentioned Nicholas's pleas in the last paragraph and his testing by the DPR as an afterthought. The reporter, who was probably some novice fresh out of college, had obviously thought the information irrelevant—as, indeed, it probably was.

The *Sun*, not untypically, had turned it all around, even though it had relegated the story to the desultory wilderness of page six. "NORMAL" BOY PREDICTS FATHER'S DEATH was the headline, and the photograph accompanying the piece was a snapshot of Nicholas, apparently two or three years out of date. Nicholas was blond, thin-faced and unsmiling, somehow rather furtive; he looked completely unlike his dark-haired, chubby and seemingly self-satisfied father.

While Simon drove on towards the suburb where the Hemdeans lived, Carol read the two articles.

"It'll be a storm in a teacup," she predicted, with more hope than certainty. "Everyone knows how many supposed Dreamers come forward for testing, and how few of them have a hit rate worth scoring."

Simon noted how carefully she had phrased the claim. Like most scientists engaged in Paranormal Studies Carol had a pet theory which she promoted in her published papers. Carol's theory was that everybody was Talented, and that intelligent life would be quite impossible without Talent; her solution of the age-old mind-body problem was that the mind was a paranormal phenomenon and that its conscious control of the body was a species of psychokinesis. In her view, classifiable Talent was only different in degree, not in kind, from everyday mental activity; anybody and everybody might therefore have the occasional precognitive insight, in a dream or any other way, and those who got to be certified Paranormals were simply those who had exceptionally accurate insights with exceptional regularity.

"It might be a bigger storm than you think," Simon told her, dolefully—and went on to tell her about Lewis Fay's proposition.

She was disgusted. "*Family Provident*," she said, as though it were an off-colour phrase. "What a ghoul! You're not thinking of doing it, are you?"

"I've already published the paper," Simon pointed out, glumly. "He was quite right—it simply had not occurred to me to think about possible practical implications. I suppose it could be given in evidence whether I agree to play ball or not. I might be summoned to testify even if I refuse the consultancy—and if I try to recant I'll look like a complete fool. And after all, it *is* conceivable that my interpretation of the precognitive paradox is the correct one."

Given the nature of Carol Cloxeter's pet theories he could not expect her to agree with his speculations, but he appealed for moral support regardless. He was not overly surprised when she simply sniffed and said "Anything's possible," in a tone which suggested that one had to be very charitable to think so.

The Hemdeans lived in a large detached house surrounded by a six-foot wall. It was a very nice house—as one might expect of the home of an architect—with big wrought-iron gates; these were guarded by a uniformed constable, who was exchanging desultory remarks with a small group of idle bystanders, some of whom carried cameras. Simon guessed that the bystanders were bored newspapermen, who knew perfectly well that they would not be allowed through the gate, but were obliged to hang about anyhow. He could not help wishing that he had a blanket to put over his head, but he took comfort from the fact that the reporters were few in number, and certainly had not the air of men on a promising assignment. A shower of rain would probably send them hurrying of in search of something spicier, and the dour November sky was obligingly threatening.

When the Mini pulled in to the gateway the newspapermen became mildly curious and the flashbulbs began to pop. The annoyed policeman bent down to order Simon to go away, but he showed his identity card and said that it was imperative that he talk to Mrs. Hemdean. The policeman—presumably a *Sun* reader—saw the logic of the situation instantly, and unfastened the gate to let the Mini through, closing it again very firmly afterwards. Simon parked the Mini behind the silver Volvo which stood outside the front door.

 Mrs. Hemdean answered the door herself. She looked at Simon with naked hostility, and perhaps a measure of distaste, but she recognised Carol and welcomed the revelation that they were not newshounds.

"Oh," she said, "it's you." She grudgingly let them in, and took them into a sitting room. "Nicholas is in bed," she said. "He's very disturbed. I honestly don't know *how* the papers got hold of the story about Nicholas being tested. One of the neighbours, I expect."

Simon sat down gingerly on the sofa. Carol sat beside him and Mrs. Hemdean lowered herself into an armchair. Mrs. Hemdean looked distressed, but not in a grief-stricken way. She was, as Carol had said, a handsome woman, and though her handsomeness was mostly gloss and grooming it had not been significantly disturbed by tragedy; her hair and make-up were perfectly in place.

"Perhaps it was the neighbour who was with you yesterday morning?" Simon suggested. "I understand that there was someone else present when Nicholas tried to prevent his father going to work."

"Oh no," said Mrs. Hemdean. "It couldn't have been *Alex.* He came to collect Debbie. She and Patricia—that's Alex's daughter—go to school together. Alex and Tom take turns dropping them off. It's quite a way, you see, and the girls daren't go past the Comprehensive while they're wearing their uniforms. Alex wouldn't have spoken to *the press.*"

Simon had felt worried about the prospect of intruding upon a widow's grief, but Mrs. Hemdean was obviously not the kind of women to let her loss disturb her manners. He couldn't help wondering whether the widow's stern composure might be more severely dented when she found out that Mr. Fay was trying to figure out a way of weaselling out of the insurance company's obligations to her.

"Can you tell us exactly what happened yesterday?" asked Simon, politely. "I know it's a terrible time to bother you, and I really don't want to cause you any further distress, but there's a chance that those reporters outside might blow the matter up out of all proportion if the mood takes them. They've already asked for a statement from the Department, and I really do need to know the full facts."

"I can't remember, exactly," said Mrs. Hemdean, unhelpfully. "Nicholas can be *so* trying at times, and one gets quite used to ignoring him. It was just another piece of nonsense He didn't say anything at breakfast, and he watched Tom get ready for work as usual. It wasn't until Alex rang the bell and Debbie answered that he began to get excited—just when everything was at its most hectic. Tom was talking to Alex in the hall—just hello, how are you, that sort of thing—and Nicholas was suddenly tugging at his trouser-leg, telling him not to go."

"Mrs. Hemdean," said Carol, gently. "It's vital that we know exactly what Nicholas said . . . what words he used. We have to know how detailed this so-called precognition was."

Mrs. Hemdean shook her head, impatiently. "I told you," she said, "I didn't really listen. I was in the kitchen when it started, and when I went into the hall my main concern was to get Nicholas away so that Tom could go to work."

"The papers claim that he foresaw every detail of the accident," Simon said, doggedly. "Personally, I find that hard to believe, given that it was such an unusual occurrence. Please try to remember, Mrs. Hemdean—did he use the word *crane* at all, or the word *tile.*"

Mrs. Hemdean clucked her tongue, and shook her head again. "He certainly said *crane,*" she said, eventually, "but I don't think he said anything about tiles."

Simon exchanged glances with Carol. They both knew that even if an eight-year-old boy had seen every detail of the accident in a dream, he might not quite understand what would have happened, and might not even know the word *tile*. The only things which would have impressed themselves strongly on his frightened mind would have been the crane dropping its load and the death of his father.

"Can we speak to Nicholas?" asked Carol.

"If he's not asleep," said Mrs. Hemdean, with a fatalistic shrug of the shoulders. "But you won't get any sense out of *him*."

As they went up the stairs, Simon said: "Mrs. Hemdean, it's obvious that neither you or your husband took this premonitory dream at all seriously—yet five months ago you brought Nicholas along to the DPR to be tested. Why did you do that, if you didn't believe he had a Talent?"

"I knew it was all nonsense," retorted Mrs. Hemdean. "It was Debbie and Tom who thought there might be something in it—Debbie was the only one who'd heard any of these so-called predictions before the accidents happened, and Tom always listens to her. Tom insisted that I bring Nicholas to you, but you only confirmed what I thought all along."

Simon frowned slightly. "So, despite the fact that your husband once thought Nicholas might have a precognitive Talent, he was still prepared to discount this particular prediction."

"I don't know about discounting it," Mrs. Hemdean said. "I couldn't get Nicholas away from him until he'd promised that he wouldn't go under the crane, but he probably just said that to keep Nicholas quiet—and anyway, he didn't go under the crane, did he?"

Perhaps he did try to negate the prophecy, thought Simon. *Perhaps he just didn't move away quite far enough!*

Nicholas wasn't asleep, but he looked in far worse shape than his mother: tired, listless, utterly stricken by grief and horror. He too remembered Carol Cloxeter, but the look he gave her was so redolent with misery and pain that Simon felt mortally uncomfortable.

At Simon's request Mrs. Hemdean left them alone, but Simon hung back while Carol sat on the bedside and took the child's hand in her own.

"I'm sorry, Nicholas," she said, "but I have to ask you some questions. Should I call you Nicholas, or Nicky?"

"My friends call me Nicky," said the boy, lifelessly. Simon noted that his mother didn't.

"Can you tell us about the dream you had?"

"I saw the crane. It was lifting something. Then it fell. It killed my daddy." As he spoke the last sentence tears welled up in the boy's eyes, but he didn't quite break down and cry.

Carol hesitated, and Simon knew that she couldn't yet bring herself to ask precisely *how* Nicky has seen his father killed. "Why didn't you say anything before?" she asked, instead. "Why did you wait until he was actually leaving the house?"

"I didn't remember until then," said the boy, miserably. "I don't always remember when I get up. Don't you remember—that's why you didn't believe me. I told you I sometimes didn't remember the dreams until after things happened. That's why mummy wouldn't believe me when she laddered her tights and when her dress got splashed. She just got mad at me, because I didn't remember the dreams till afterwards. This time, I remembered in time . . . but she wouldn't believe me anyway. Nobody believed me, except Debbie. You didn't."

"It wasn't that I didn't believe you," said Carol, forlornly. "It's just that . . . we have to be very sure, you see. There are so many people who think they have a Talent, and so few who really can do anything extraordinary. It's not easy to tell, sometimes." She turned uncomfortably to face Simon. "I'll carry on here," she said. "Maybe you should ask Mrs. Hemdean about . . . other possibilities."

Simon nodded, and was ashamed to find himself rather relieved as he descended the staircase and went in search of Nicholas's mother. The "other possibilities" which he had to ask about were, of course, psychokinetic incidents. If his own theory were true, and Nicholas had unconsciously engineered the events which he had earlier "dreamed", they were unlikely to have been the only evidences of his capricious Talent.

He tried to tackle the subject in a roundabout way, but Mrs. Hemdean was no fool. She couldn't know why he was asking, but she knew what it was that he was fishing for. "Of course things sometimes fall down," she said, snappily. "Of course they break. Accidents happen. But no matter how infuriating Nicholas can be, I'm not such a fool as to think he's responsible. It's annoying when he tells me that he knew something was going to happen, but he doesn't mean any harm. We're no more accident-prone than any other family, and we certainly don't have a *poltergeist* in the house. Look around you, Mr. Sweetland—do you think I'd keep ornaments like these about the house if things were always getting hurled through the air?"

Simon surveyed the knickknacks on the sideboard and the mantelpiece. They weren't antique Dresden, but they weren't cheap either. *No specific evidence, however weak, of psychokinesis,* he thought, making notes in anticipation of a possible cross-examination. *No evidence whatsoever—I hope—that there was any antagonism between the boy and his father . . . in fact, in his shoes, I'd have been more inclined to drop a concrete pile on his mother.* He blushed at the last thought, but Mrs. Hemdean didn't notice. He wondered whether he ought to tell her about Mr. Fay, but decided against it, not knowing whether to call the decision diplomacy or cowardice.

Carol was a long time coming down, and when she did eventually come down she wasn't alone.

"This is Debbie," said Carol, introducing her companion to Simon; Simon had already guessed—the young girl was stamped from exactly the same mould as her mother. Her school uniform was uncannily neat, despite that she seemed so unhappy. Simon saw from the corner of his eye that Mrs. Hemdean was only very slightly annoyed to see Carol and her daughter together; she obviously had no particular worries about anything that Debbie might have said.

"Debbie's the only person Nicky always tells when he has his dreams," said Carol, more for the girl's benefit than Simon's. "She says that when he tells her something's going to happen to her, she makes sure it doesn't. She says that he's never let her down."

In other words, thought Simon, *she knows he was right because what he said would happen didn't, although it might have if he hadn't warned her.* It was the precognitive paradox in all its glory.

"I did tell Daddy to be careful," said Debbie, mournfully. "I thought that would be enough. I thought that if he knew about the crane, he wouldn't be in any danger. He did promise—he did." She too was on the brink of tears. Only Mrs. Hemdean was immune.

"The papers seem to have got it wrong," said Carol. "Debbie remembers quite clearly what Nicky said—he never said anything about shattered fragments flying about; he only said that the crane would drop something, and that his father would fall down. Mr. Hemdean thought he would be safe, if only he was careful not to get underneath the crane . . . which he probably wouldn't have done anyhow."

"We'll have to make that clear," said Simon, mechanically, for Mrs. Hemdean's benefit.

"And we'll have to test Nicky again, when he's well enough to be tested," said Carol, also speaking for Mrs. Hemdean's ears rather than his. "Just to make sure."

"Yes," said Simon, hollowly. "Just to make sure." He had a feeling that Mrs. Hemdean might not be very keen on that idea, when she found out what Mr. Fay had up his sleeve. In fact, he had a feeling that Mrs. Hemdean would be decidedly unready to speak to him—or anyone else from the DPR—ever again. He only hoped that she wouldn't decide that the idea of talking to the press wasn't so hideous after all; there was nothing more likely to keep a tabloid story running than a rich source of spiteful accusations.

But there was nothing he could do but wait and see what happened.

* * *

"What do you think?" asked Simon, unhappily, as he drove back to the DPR building.

"Neither of the kids said anything to lend support to the idea that he's a subconscious psychokinetic," she said, bluntly. "And we also have to bear in mind that he was seven miles away from the scene of the supposed subconscious crime. How many PKs do you know who could direct the flight of a fragment of a tile at that sort of distance?

Simon sighed. "One of the Gods could do it," he said, "but none of our Temps could, that's for sure."

"At this point in time," she said, mildly, "I certainly wouldn't swap my pet theory for yours."

"I don't blame you," he said. "Do you think he really is a precog?"

She looked at him as if she were Sherlock Holmes saying "You know my methods, Watson, apply them!" What she actually said was: "We all have precognitive flashes, Simon. It's just that most of us don't remember them, don't trust them or call them coincidences. The sort of evidence which convinced Debbie could be produced by almost anyone. If the boy does have an out-of-the-ordinary Talent he'll have to get far better control of it before we could take him on."

"Maybe you'd better write the press release," he said, bitterly.

"You're welcome to quote me," she assured him, looking and sounding rather smug. Then, after a pause, she said: "Don't worry about Fay. He won't dare to play his malicious games unless he has your active support—insurance companies have to be pretty sure of their ground before they put their public image at risk. Even if he does, you can always use the King James defence."

"What the hell's that?" he asked.

She looked faintly surprised that he didn't know. "James the First wrote a book on witchcraft, arguing in favour of the case that witches did exist—but every time he got involved with an actual witch trial after he became king of England he had the charges dismissed, on the grounds that although witchcraft was real, it played no part in the particular cases in question. So, you can still stick to your theory if you want—all you have to say is that this isn't an instance of it."

Simon knew that she was only trying to let him off the hook, but he also knew that it would still be going back on his argument. *Her* view was that precognition was real, but that this particular instance of it was no big deal; *he* had argued in print that the idea of precognition, given its paradoxical implications was logically untenable, and that *all* the supposed examples of it might be explicable as mistaken psychokinesis. The "might be" had certainly been cautious enough, but there was no way he could worm his way out of the "logically untenable". He had stuck his neck out, knowing at the time that he was being slightly daring, but actually feeling rather pleased with himself. Now the axe was falling. If he turned around now and said that perhaps there was real precognition after all, he was going to look very silly indeed. Lewis Fay had seen that clearly enough—and that was why Fay had thought it worth the trouble to offer him a consultancy.

When they got back to the DPR, keeping the lone waiting reporter at bay with promises of a statement to come, they found Marcia glued to the portable TV which she kept under her desk—which was, Simon supposed, marginally preferable to finding her glued to the telephone. She was watching the local news, on which a building contractor in an orange safety-helmet was explaining how extremely unfortunate poor Thomas Hemdean had been.

"It was a chance in a million," he said. "Never seen one like it before, and I don't expect ever to see one like it again. But accidents do happen. When you put up big buildings, you get falls and breakages—and the bigger the building is, the more likely it is that someone will get killed. A lot of the lads are superstitious—they get premonitions too, you know, and the company has a couple of Talented troubleshooters of its own—but in the end, you just can't cover all the angles. Least of all the million-to-one-shots."

Marcia looked up when Simon and Carol paused. "Isn't it marvellous?" she said. "That little boy knowing *exactly* what would happen to his father, even after you said that he was perfectly normal. It just goes to show that you never can tell."

As Simon trudged upstairs to his office he felt as though his feet were lined with lead. He was not looking forward to writing a statement for the press, and he was *certainly* not looking forward to facing Mr. Fay again.

It seemed like such a good idea at the time, he thought.

He worded the release with the utmost care, pointing out that Nicholas Hemdean's warning had in fact been rather vague, and reiterating that there had been and was insufficient evidence to support the hypothesis that Nicholas had *any* kind of Paranormal Talent, but it seemed feeble even to him, and he knew that it wouldn't satisfy the press if they decided to follow up on the story.

It was not merely his and Carol's promotion prospects which were under threat, he knew, but also his own intellectual self-respect. But when he thought of Nicholas Hemdean's miserable face, he knew that he could not possibly follow the course which Lewis Fay had proposed. There was no way in the world that he could ever say, if asked, that Nicholas might actually have brought about the death of his father. Such a thing could not be said, and could not even be thought—not because it could not be true, but because it would be far too cruel.

Silently, Simon turned in his chair and plucked the latest issue of the *Journal of Paranormal Studies* from his bookshelf. He dropped it in the bin. Then he took his phone off the hook and got on with his work.

* * *

By the time five-thirty rolled around, mercifully without further incident, Simon was feeling a little better. It seemed that the storm in a teacup had already blown itself out, and he had convinced himself that the newspapers would drop the story. Then, just as he was about to leave, Carol Cloxeter came hurrying into his office, waving a fax.

She no longer looked smug. In fact, she looked somewhat shaken.

"Simon," she said. "Look at this!"

He scanned the piece of paper quickly. It was from a firm of solicitors, Montgomery & Clift, notifying Carol of the intention of Mrs. Elizabeth

Hemdean to file a suit against her and the DPR for compensatory damages in respect of the death of her husband—which, alleged the fax, could have been prevented if Carol had not been negligent in failing to establish the precognitive abilities of Nicholas Hemdean. A second copy had been sent to the Division Head, but had presumably arrived too late to be seen by him—yet.

"They're crazy!" said Simon. "There's no way in the world they can make it stick."

"Maybe not," said Carol. "But the fact that they intend to try will be enough to promote the story from page six to page one, and we're going to look very bad indeed."

Simon frowned. "But it doesn't make any sense," he said. "When we saw Mrs. Hemdean this morning she didn't show the slightest sign of thinking that we might be to blame—and she seemed determined to hold on to the belief that Nicholas *isn't* a precog. What changed her mind?"

"Mr. Fay?" suggested Carol, in a tone which was nakedly accusative. Clearly she thought that Simon's heretical opinions had now rebounded upon her. He winced at the thought that she might be right.

"You think he's told her that there might be a problem with her insurance claim, and that she's decided to get her retaliation in first?"

"What else?"

Simon found the card with the record of Nicholas's tests, and checked the telephone number recorded there. When he got an engaged tone he guessed immediately that he was not the only one who had thought it politic to be unreachable.

"Get your coat," he said, with unusual decisiveness. "We'll go round there again."

"Is that wise?" she asked.

"Probably not," he admitted. "But there's just a chance we can get this cleared up if I tell her that I haven't the slightest intention of backing up Fay's gambit. If she knows the insurance claim will be met, perhaps she'll be prepared to abandon this nonsense before she contrives to ruin the pair of us."

It had finally begun to rain, and the sky was so heavy with cloud that it was nearly dark. The raindrops drumming on the roof of the Mini as it ploughed its weary way through the last vestiges of the rush hour sounded dreadfully ominous, but Simon's weak attempts to start a conversation were stonewalled by his anxious companion. Although he knew that he was not really to blame for the deepening mess that they were in, Simon could not help but feel horribly guilty. There was nothing in the world he hated more than to have Carol's displeasure aimed in his direction.

The rain had, as he had earlier hoped, driven off the reporters and the cameramen, and the dutiful policeman was looking distinctly bedraggled as he tried to make the most of the inadequate shelter offered by a sullen sycamore. When he recognised them he simply waved them on, clearly in no mood to question their right of access. The parking space in the driveway was severely constricted by a black BMW which had joined the still-ungaraged Volvo, but Simon managed to squeeze the Mini in.

When he rang the doorbell Simon had awful visions of the door being promptly slammed in their faces by an angry widow, but in fact it was Debbie Hemdean who answered the door, in the company of another girl of similar age, dressed in a similar school uniform.

"Please come in," said Debbie, scrupulously. "This is my friend Patricia Clift." She waited until Simon had dutifully wiped his feet on the mat, then shouted: "Mummy, it's the lady and gentleman who came to see us this morning."

By the time that Elizabeth Hemdean had arrived at the sitting-room door, Simon was practically through it. The widow did indeed look wrathful, and it was evident that they might indeed have had trouble obtaining admittance had she come to the door in person, but the reflexes of polite hospitality made her stand back now that the unwelcome guests were actually inside. She was not alone; there was a man sitting on the sofa on which Simon and Carol had earlier perched—a tall, slim man with piercing blue eyes.

"Alex," said the flustered Mrs. Hemdean. "These are the people I told you about . . . "

"The people you rather suddenly decided to sue," said Simon, surprised at his own acidity. He quickly put two and two together and extended his hand to the stranger. "Mr. Clift, I assume," he said. "Of Montgomery & Clift, no doubt."

While Mrs. Hemdean ushered the two schoolgirls from the room, shepherding them towards the staircase, the tall man accepted the proffered hand and shook it disdainfully. "My firm represents Mrs. Hemdean," he agreed. "In the circumstances, Mr . . . er . . . I am rather surprised to see you here."

"Sweetland," said Simon, unabashed. "*Doctor* Sweetland. This is Dr. Cloxeter, against whom you seem to intend issuing some kind of writ. And we're here because we don't quite understand what the circumstances are. Was it *your* idea to proceed with this action?"

"I have advised Mrs. Hemdean of her rights, of course," said Clift, smoothly, glancing towards the lady as she returned to the room and shut the door behind her. "I shall not be handling the case personally, of course, because I may be required to appear as a witness."

"A witness?" repeated Simon, with a distinct edge in his voice. "And I suppose that you—unlike Mrs. Hemdean—have a perfect recollection of what Nicholas said to his father in the hall."

"I have," agreed Clift, serenely. "I heard the prophecy uttered, and I saw its fulfilment. I can testify to its accuracy in every particular, and can say without hesitation that if only Tom Hemdean had not been assured that his son had no precognitive ability, he would never have taken the risk of going on site today—-he would have been a beneficiary of what I believe you call the Oedipus effect."

Simon was slightly flustered by this further revelation.

"You saw the accident, too?" he queried.

"Certainly. I was meeting Tom for lunch—partly social, partly business. I had just driven on to the site to pick him up when I saw the pile begin to fall. I could see Tom quite clearly, and I saw him fall when the fragment of tile struck him."

"But Nicholas didn't say anything about a fragment of tile, did he?" said Simon. "He *didn't* foresee what happened—not exactly."

"I'm afraid," said Clift, icily, "that it would be most irregular for me to discuss with you and Dr. Cloxeter the nature of the evidence which I may be required to give in court. And I must say that I see no point whatsoever in your continued presence here."

The expression on Alex Clift's face was by no means a smile, but it had in it that same superciliousness that Simon had earlier seen in Lewis Fay's face. "I'm a lawyer," it said, "and you're only some dumb scientific civil servant. I can run rings around you." Simon guessed that he and Carol had jumped to the wrong conclusion about what had brought this on. This was simply one more clever bastard with an eye to the main chance—and that, he realised, might give him an opportunity to dispel that look from Alex Clift's face.

While his resolve was hardening into anger, Simon turned to look at

Mrs. Hemdean, who was still hovering near the door. "You know that Nicholas didn't say anything about a tile, Mrs. Hemdean," he said, levelly. "Neither Nicholas nor Debbie remembered him saying any such thing when we talked to them this morning."

Mrs. Hemdean wouldn't meet his eye. "I'm sure Alex remembers far better than the children what was said," she told him. "I was distracted, but he is perfectly reliable in such matters."

Simon turned back to Clift. "Do you know a man named Lewis Fay?" he asked, bluntly.

Clift was obviously surprised to be asked, and Simon was glad to see it. "Slightly," said Clift. "He's a member at my golf club, but not a friend."

"Do you know what he does for a living?" Simon asked.

"Not really," said Clift, warily. "I think he's with Family Provident."

"He's a claims assessor with Family Provident," Simon amplified. "He came to see me this morning, about Mr. Hemdean's life insurance."

Simon took considerable satisfaction from the sight of Clift's guarded surprise changing to open astonishment. He glanced sideways at Carol, but she simply looked worried. She didn't believe the ploy would work, and she was scared of storing up even more trouble.

"What about Tom's life insurance?" said Mrs. Hemdean, suddenly coming forward to stand beside Clift, facing Simon and Carol. The hostility of the four stares seemed almost tangible.

"You're not the only ones who had a bright idea about using this case to establish a precedent," said Simon, with a humourless smile. "Would you care to sit down, while I tell you what he said to me?"

They all sat down. It seemed to take a little of the tension out of the air, but not one of them sat comfortably. Briefly, Simon told them the substance of his article, and the opportunity which Lewis Fay had read between its lines. While he did so, he watched Alex Clift's expression become even frostier.

"You'll never get away with it," he told Simon, when the substance of the argument had been made clear. "You could never prove it."

"Mr. Fay seems to think that strict proof isn't necessary," Simon countered. "He seems to think that it might be enough simply to create a doubt in people's minds. You should be able to sympathize—after all, *you* can't possibly hope to prove that Carol was negligent in testing Nicholas; you could only succeed in sowing enough seeds of doubt to encourage the Department to settle out of court rather than risk a jury's decision."

Clift stared at him for half a minute, then said: "Are you trying to make a deal, Dr. Sweetland? Are you offering to refrain from alleging that Nicholas may have subconsciously caused the death of his father in return for our dropping the suit against your colleague?"

Simon looked sideways at Carol again, but she was almost expressionless, waiting to see what would happen. He looked back at Clift, meeting the bright blue eyes squarely.

"No," he said, "I'm not. I don't think you'd accept the offer, and I think you might try to use the fact that I'd made it against us."

Clift grinned, sure of himself now whether he had been sure before or not. "You're right, Dr. Sweetland," he said. "We would have fought you to the death—and we'd have won. Not only because your case is lousy at the logical level but because you wouldn't stand a chance with a jury if you tried to nail an eight-year-old boy for causing his father's death. Tom loved that boy, and the boy loved Tom. We would have made you look very sick, Dr. Sweetland. Very sick."

Then he smiled, in sharklike fashion.

Carol was staring unhappily at the floor.

"On the other hand," said Simon, without a trace of emotion in his voice, "I'd still like your assurance that you won't proceed with this fatuous suit against Dr. Cloxeter."

"I'm afraid that I can't give you any such assurance," said Clift. He was obviously not a man to refrain from seizing and retaining any and all initiatives. "It is still our intention to proceed. And now, I think, we have no more to say to one another." He came to his feet as he spoke.

"You're wrong," said Simon, flatly. "If I leave here without your guarantee, I shall go straight to Lewis Fay."

"But you just said . . . " Clift began.

Simon stood up so that he could look the man as nearly in the eye as the disparity in their heights would permit. "I just agreed that I had no intention of going into a witness box in order to claim that Nicholas might have killed his father. All the evidence says that he not only didn't do it, but couldn't have. But it so happens, Mr. Clift, that I really do believe what I wrote in my article. I believe that precognition is logically untenable, and that what we think are cases of successful precognition are actually cases of subconscious psychokinesis. I know that Nicholas didn't cause Thomas Hemdean's death, Mr. Clift—but I don't know that *you* didn't."

The colour drained from Alex Clift's features. Mrs. Hemdean sprang to her feet, and Carol belatedly stood up too.

"You're mad!" said Clift, loudly.

"Am I?" Simon retorted, wishing that he was as calm as he was trying to sound. "If I were in the witness box, Mr. Clift—and I'm sorry if it's irregular to give you advance notice of my testimony—I would have to point out several things. Firstly, Nicholas only became agitated about the danger to his father when you and your daughter came to pick Debbie up in order to take her to school. He *thought* that he was remembering a dream he'd had, but perhaps he wasn't. He isn't, so far as we can tell, a precog—but we haven't tested him for telepathy. Secondly, you were present at the scene of the accident; you've just told me that you saw the pile fall, and that you saw Thomas Hemdean struck down. No PK I know could have affected the flight of that piece of tile from several miles away, but I know three or four right here in Coventry who could have done it from where you were sitting."

"I didn't have any reason for wanting Tom Hemdean dead," said Clift, uneasily.

"Maybe not *consciously*," said Simon. "But I don't have to prove anything, remember? I only have to sow the seeds of doubt. Of course, you'd have every opportunity to demonstrate your lack of motive. You'd undoubtedly be able to prove beyond a shadow of a doubt that all your business dealings with Thomas Hemdean were above board—after all, you're a friend of the family, aren't you?—and I'm just as certain as you are that genetic fingerprinting would prove that in spite of superficial appearances, Nicholas really is Thomas Hemdean's son, and not yours."

Clift's pallor had become almost ghastly. "You say that in court and I'll crucify you!" he said.

"I won't have to say it in court, will I, Mr. Clift?" said Simon, drily. "I won't even have to confide it, off the record, to the man from the *Sun*—because in the morning, this will all have died down, won't it? No writs, no fuss, no story. *Now*, I think, we have nothing further to say to one another."

Without another word, Simon turned and marched to the door. He held it open while Carol passed through, and looked back at Alex Clift and Elizabeth Hemdean, who were staring after him.

"Don't bother to show us out," he said. "We know the way."

Not until he was at the front door did he glance back again. Neither Clift nor Mrs. Hemdean had come out into the hall, but at the top of the staircase, just visible above the rail of the bannister as it curved around the corner, were three faces in a line. The one in the middle was Nicholas Hemdean, who was watching him with mournful eyes. There was, of course, no way that the three children could have overheard what was said, but Simon shivered anyhow as he closed the door behind him.

He could not put away the memory of those mournful eyes while he drove Carol Cloxeter home through the driving rain. He dropped her outside the gate of her neat semi, and watched her as she hurried up the path. He saw the glass-fronted door open to welcome her even before she reached it. Then he went on to the empty flat which awaited him.

* * *

Simon was to remember that face, and those eyes, three days later when he stopped on his way home to pick up an evening paper, and read a minor headline which said: **LOCAL SOLICITOR KILLED IN FREAK ACCIDENT.**

According to the story, Alexander Clift had been on a shopping trip to the city centre. He had driven his BMW to the top floor of a multi-storey car park, stopping briefly near the lifts to let out his passengers: a friend and her two children, and his own daughter. Then he had driven on a little way, and had begun to manoeuvre the big car rear-first into a narrow parking-space.

Somehow—perhaps by hitting the accelerator instead of the brake—the driver had overshot the mark. The reinforced concrete parapet which should have stopped the car had crumbled away in spite of the low impact speed, and the car had somehow gone over the edge.

A spokesman for NCP, which owned and operated the car park, said that the failure of the parapet to stop the car was quite inexplicable. "Our car parks are perfectly safe," he was quoted as saying. "This was a million-to-one-shot. No one could have possibly have anticipated it. We will make certain that it can never happen again."

The names of the other passengers were not given. Nor, for that matter, was the name of the architect who had designed the car park. Presumably the reporter, who was probably a novice not long out of college, considered such details irrelevant—as, indeed, they probably were.

SORTILEGE AND SERENDIPITY

Of all the words in all the world, the ones which Simon Sweetland most dreaded to hear were: "This is Ramsbottom in Accounts. Could you possibly spare me a few minutes to discuss your recent claim for expenses?"

In the eleven years he had worked as a tester for DPR Coventry Simon had heard those words—*exactly* those words, spoken in exactly the same reedy voice—more than a dozen times, and they had always been a prelude to embarrassment, awkwardness and downright misery. By now, he had become conditioned; the moment he heard the fatal syllables his stomach would contract to the size and texture of a cricket ball and he would break out into a cold sweat.

This time, he had known that it was going to happen. In fact, he had been apprehensive about the call for two days, since the claim for the Paris trip had gone in. Every time the telephone had rung his symptoms had gone through a rapid ready-steady, poised for "go", and every time he had heard the soft huskiness of Carol Cloxeter's voice—or even Marcia's petulant whine—instead of the fatal incantation, the abrupt relaxation had left him weak and confused. When he finally heard the words of doom he was so strung out that he was almost glad to know that the waiting was over.

Almost.

He knew that it was going to be worse this time than ever before. As he trudged down the stone staircase, wondering at the cruel irony of fate which had located Ramsbottom's lair directly below his own office in the two-storey annexe which Testing and Accounts shared, he wished that he had never accepted the invitation to attend the conference, that the invitation had never been made, that the conference had never been planned, that the United Kingdom had never joined the EEC, that there was no such city as Paris . . .

Ramsbottom was sitting behind his desk as he always was: a tiny ratty little man with an absurd moustache which somehow reminded Simon of Hitler's, H. G. Wells's and Charlie Chaplin's, all rolled into one. When Simon had first seen Ramsbottom many years before the accountant had been lurking behind massive piles of box-files arrayed like battlements on his desk, but Ramsbottom believed in moving with the times. Nowadays he skulked behind a trio of computer-terminals which not only kept the world at bay but bathed his face in an eerie green glow. Although Ramsbottom's office was exactly the same size as Simon's it seemed much smaller because of the vast stacks of files piled high against every wall; they were all obsolete now that the ingenious Ramsbottom had computerised the entire Midlands Division system (five years ahead of the official time-target) but the DPR, like most branches of the civil service, had strong taboos against throwing things away. The hulking masses of ancient paper always made Ramsbottom's den seem dingy and disgusting, although the cleaners presumably went in every morning to to give it the despairing stare which was all that NUPE's new demarcation rules permitted them to do.

"Please sit down, Dr Sweetland," said Ramsbottom. Simon imagined that Torquemada must have used exactly the same tone when inviting his victims to stretch themselves out on the rack.

"There's nothing irregular in our claim," Simon said, pre-emptively, as he took his allotted place. "All the receipts are there."

"They are indeed," Ramsbottom agreed, riffling through the papers in his hand. Travel receipts from Thomas Cook, bill for two rooms for five nights at the Hotel Trianon, five restaurant bills, receipts for three journeys by taxi. A very full account of your stay, if I may say so. Very full indeed."

Simon explained, mostly without being directly asked, why he and Carol had stayed at the Trianon instead of a cheaper hotel (because it was within walking distance of the Sorbonne, where the conference had been held), why he and Carol, had taken the taxis instead of using the airport bus or the Metro (problems with timing), and why two of the five restaurant bills were for *à la carte* instead of set meals. He was morally certain that his position was unassailable, and that the very best Ramsbottom could do would be to disqualify a couple of the restaurant bills, but he still felt crushed by the awful pressure of having to justify himself.

"It was an important conference," he finished, lamely. "The First EC Symposium on Paranormality. It was a great honour to be invited. You must have read the memos London has been sending round about the importance of 1992 and the necessity of thinking European. We were there representing our country." He threw in the last bit because he suspected that Ramsbottom might be the patriotic type, although it was entirely probable that the accountant's allegiance was to the pound sterling rather than the Queen. If only Ramsbottom were in charge of the Civil List!

"Was it absolutely necessary for Mrs Cloxeter to accompany you to Paris?" Ramsbottom asked, mournfully contemplating the total displayed on his left-hand screen.

"It was a joint paper," Simon pointed out. "We were equal co-authors."

"It might take two people to write a paper," Ramsbottom observed, lugubriously. "But it only takes one to read it."

My god, Simon thought, as the accountant's beady little eyes seared him with disapproval. *He thinks that I took Carol over there for a dirty weekend! He actually thinks we were having it away. And the reason he finds that such an appalling thought is not because Carol's married—it's because he thinks we could have saved on the hotel bill by only booking one room!*

Ramsbottom's suspicion—all the more deadly for being unspoken—made Simon feel horribly guilty, not because he and Carol had actually done anything, but rather because he'd spent the greater part of his time in Paris fervently but hopelessly wishing that they might.

"We were both invited," Simon said, as frigidly as he could. "And we were both given leave to go. I think you'll find that everything is in order."

Ramsbottom put the receipts down and brought something else out of the mysterious depths behind his high-tech ramparts. Simon recognised it as a copy of the souvenir programme which had been issued to all the participants in the conference. It contained heavily abridged versions of all the papers which had been presented—the fuller versions, with all the statistical appendices, would appear in a much bulkier volume of *Proceedings* in nine months time.

"Your contribution to this volume," said Ramsbottom, accusatively, "is called 'Sortilege and Serendipity', I believe."

"Well," said Simon, warily, "We actually titled our paper 'Experienced locality effects and the inverse square-law as key variables affecting the effective range of talents for discovery, and the significant differences pertaining to sortilege and serendipity' but the editor felt that the full thing was a bit cumbersome, so he cut it down."

There was a brief but pregnant silence. It was broken by the sound of a door opening and closing, followed by the sound of footsteps crossing a floor. Simon knew that it was the door to his own office, but curiosity about the identity of the person who had entered (the footfalls had not been those of Carol's high-heeled shoes) was drowned out by painful consciousness of the fact that every day, year in and year out, Ramsbottom could hear every move he made. Simon knew that Ramsbottom always stayed late, and therefore always knew to the minute exactly what time he went home. There was no earthly reason why that information should be secret, but somehow it was exceedingly uncomfortable to know that Ramsbottom had it.

"Dr Sweetland," said Ramsbottom, tiredly, "Were you and Mrs Cloxeter *paid* for your contribution to this volume?"

Simon felt his throat go suddenly dry. In all his eleven years with the DPR, it was the first time he had ever been paid for a publication, and he could not help feeling a fit of panic at the horrid thought that he had done something wrong, and that Ramsbottom knew about it. It was pure paranoia, but Ramsbottom always had that effect on him.

"It's allowed," he said, squeakily. "We don't have to pay it into Department funds. We checked. It's ours. It was only five hundred francs, divided between the two of us."

"I am aware," said Ramsbottom, frostily, "that the Department has no *legal* claim on the fee which you and Mrs Cloxeter received for this publication. I merely wondered whether you might not feel a *moral responsibility* to put the fee towards your expenses. As you are well aware, the Department is funded by the *British taxpayers*, and has a *responsibility* to those taxpayers to make absolutely certain that it disperses its funds in an economical and constructive fashion. I merely felt that as a matter of *conscience* and *duty* to the good people of this country you might feel it *appropriate* to waive a portion of your expenses in recognition of this fee—which you received, after all, as a direct result of your participation in the conference."

Simon felt that all the slings and arrows of outrageous fortune were being hurled upon him with lethal force and deadly accuracy. Ramsbottom's green-tinged face, with three lighted screens reflected in each dark, accusing eye, seemed absolutely diabolical. He opened his mouth to reply, but no words came.

"Shall I take that as a yes?" said Ramsbottom, malevolently.

Simon wanted to say "no". He wanted to shout, to scream, or to bellow "no". He would have given his right arm—or, at any rate, one of his little fingers—for the moral courage to say: "Damn your eyes, Ramsbottom, if you don't get your sticky sanctimonious paws off my legitimate expenses I'll feed you feet first to the shredder." But it was no good. Even though he was already wondering how he was going to explain it to Carol, he knew that he was beaten. He was not usually an *absolute* coward, but when confronted by Ramsbottom he was a wimp before a weasel, an ant beneath an aardvark's snout.

When he finally managed to persuade his larynx to unfreeze, all that came out was a strangled "Awk!"

"Thank you, Dr Sweetland," said Ramsbottom. "I knew that we could get things straightened out, with a little good will on both sides. At heart, you see, we're both men of good conscience."

The accountant never even smiled. In all the eleven years he had known him, Simon had never once seen Ramsbottom smile, even in victory.

* * *

When he staggered back into his own office, Simon was momentarily startled to find someone sitting in the chair where loving parents usually sat while watching their offspring strut their stuff. The traumatic effects of Ramsbottom's coup had driven the little mystery of who had gone into his office clean out of his mind.

Simon quickly controlled his momentary alarm. The man looked utterly nondescript and quite harmless. His placid, clean-shaven features were far less menacing than Ramsbottom's, and he wore a neat grey gaberdine raincoat of a distinctly unfashionable type.

The visitor came swiftly to his feet as Simon crossed to the desk, extending an ID card which he had evidently been holding in readiness for the moment of presentation. Simon took it, read it, and gasped. Appearances were, it seemed, deceptive. The ID revealed that his visitor was Inspecteur de la s—ret, Jean Croupion, on secondment to the

Marseilles division of Interpol. Simon had never seen an Interpol ID card before, and was appropriately impressed. He conscientiously checked the photograph to make sure that it fit the face of the man who stood before him.

"Monsieur Sweetland?" said Croupion, in a tone which sounded all the more conspiratorial for being strongly accented.

"I'm Dr Sweetland," Simon confirmed. The other appeared to be waiting for something, but it took several seconds before the penny dropped. "Oh, sorry," he said, fumbling for his wallet, where he kept his own ID. The after-effects of his meeting with Ramsbottom combined with his present embarrassment to make him drop the wallet. His ID card fell out, along with his Access card and his public library borrowers' card. Croupion bent down to recover them for him, glancing at them as he handed them back.

"Is not zat I doubt you," he said, softly. "But zese days, one 'as to be careful, and zis is a matter of ze utmost delicacy. May I presume that you 'ave signed what in your country ze *Official Secrets Act?*"

"Of course I have," Simon told him. "*Everybody* in the Scientific Civil Service has to sign the Official Secrets Act."

"Zen I must tell you zat everyzing which passes between us is to be kept in ze strictest confidence. It is not merely ze security of Angleterre which is at stake, but ze security of all Europe. I am investigating a crime of formidable dimension."

Just as Croupion finished his melodramatic announcement there was a knock on the door, and Simon jumped, almost dropping his wallet for a second time. Carol Cloxeter came in without waiting for an answer, as she always did when she knew that he didn't have any testing appointments. Croupion's right hand made a nervous gesture in the direction of his left armpit, but the move was quickly stilled.

"It's okay," Simon assured the Interpol man. "This is my assistant, Carol Cloxeter." *Who presumably wants to know*, he added, silently, *how I got on with the repulsive Ramsbottom.*

"Ah, but of course!" Croupion said. "The co-author of your excellent paper on sortilege and serendipity!"

Simon blinked, not knowing whether to feel extremely flattered or slightly worried. He and Carol had experienced some difficulty in France because the French language had no word for serendipity and the French word *sortilège* had such broad connotations that it tended to be almost synonymous with *magic* rather than referring narrowly to talents for finding things, as it had conventionally come to do in the pages of the British *Journal of Paranormal Studies*. If Croupion was here to find out whether Simon and Carol could help Interpol solve some particularly heinous crime, he might well be labouring under some sort of delusion.

"I'm afraid that the short version isn't as clear as it might be," Simon said, quickly. "Although the case-studies we cited involved some fairly talented youngsters, the whole point of our investigation was that they could only find things *in Coventry*. Most of the kids we test can only find things in the street where they live. We really aren't in a position to help track down international jewel-thieves or drug-smugglers. Surely External Relations explained that to you."

"Monsieur Sweetland," said the man in the gaberdine, putting a reassuring hand on Simon's shoulder, "I 'ave not talked to your External Relations. I 'ave come straight to you. No one must know I am 'ere, or zat I 'ave been 'ere. Zat is most vital. What I am looking for is in Coventry—I am certain of zat. I 'ave read your paper most carefully, and it 'as given me new 'ope. Zis boy you refer to, 'oom you call *sujet Ash* . . . I zink 'e is perfect for my purpose. I *must* see 'im."

It took Simon fully ten seconds to works out that *sujet Ash* was French for subject H. "But that's young Tommy Ferris," he blurted out. "The Phone Freak Kid." In saying this he casually broke all the Department's rules about confidentiality and violated all the conventions regarding the use of derogatory nicknames. Tommy Ferris's name had that effect on him—the child was a tester's nightmare, always throwing in fake and supposedly funny answers in order to wind people up. That was hard enough to tolerate in people with Talents which might one day prove useful, but in Tommy's case it was particularly vexing because his Talent had always seemed virtually useless, all the more so because the wild goose chases on which he delighted to send the people who sent to check out his claims could be very time-consuming.

Tommy's Talent was one of the silliest Simon had ever encountered. If you gave him the receiver of any telephone in Coventry, and a local street-map, he could unerringly find the present location of—but could not actually identify by name—every single person who had used the phone in the previous ten days, provided that they were still in the city. If he had only been able to recall the substance of their conversations, or even if he had been able to operate anywhere outside his home town, there might have been a role for him to play in the Department's activities, but as things stood there seemed little future for the lad except for tracking down the occasional dirty phone-caller. Tommy would probably be taken on to the books when he was old enough, provided that his Talent hadn't vanished with the onset of puberty, but the chances of ever finding him a useful job to do had seemed remote.

"He can't locate the users of *any* telephone," Simon said, certain that the Interpol man must be labouring under a misapprehension. "Beyond a seven-mile radius of his home his Talent suffers a steep decline in effectiveness. And the people he locates have to be within the same seven-mile radius. Our paper argues that the seven-mile limit results from a combination of his familiarity with the actual places involved and an inverse-square effect like that governing such field-effects as gravity. Maybe when he's older he can relocate to somewhere more interesting, but transplanted Talents of this general kind don't usually recover their original power and accuracy."

"Ze man we are after is in Coventry," said Croupion, confidently. "And we know for a fact that 'e 'as used a particular public telephone. We 'ave traced 'is calls, but 'e is a clever devil—'e uses ze phone only to emit a signal which triggers . . . but I cannot reveal zat. You must take me to *sujet Ash* wizout delay. It is of ze utmost importance."

"Well," said Simon, dubiously, wondering what possible interest Interpol could have in phone calls made from a public phone in Coventry. "Tommy isn't actually a Temp, you know. He's too young. We do call on the services of juvenile Talents when it's absolutely necessary, but the Department rules are very strict about chaperoning."

"I understand zis," said Croupion, who was beginning to show distinct signs of exasperation. "Per'aps you or zis charming lady will volunteer to be *le chaperon*. Zis is a matter of great urgency. More zan life and death is at stake—it is a matter of *international relations*. All Europe will have cause to zank *sujet Ash*, if he can tell us what we need to know, I promise you zat."

"Will there be any expense involved?" asked Simon, warily, with a guilty sidelong glance in Carol's direction.

"Absolutely not," said the inspector. "I 'ave 'ired a car. No problem."

Even Carol had now begin to show signs of impatience. "I'll do it," she said. "I've got no appointments, and I can handle Tommy."

Simon blushed at the accuracy of her divination. His hatred of practical jokes was such that he would be very happy if he never again clapped eyes on Tommy Ferris as long as he lived. Carol knew that—as, of course, did

Tommy, who had naturally added Simon to his list of favourite targets.

"Oh, all right then," he said. He added, with as much sarcasm as he could muster, "Give my regards to Tommy."

"All Europe would zank you, Monsieur Sweetland," Croupion assured him, "if zey knew what you 'ad done for zem. If you please, Madame Cloxeter . . . " He was already holding the door open for her.

Simon stood still for a while after they had gone, wondering what on earth was going on. He wished that he could have demanded a fuller explanation, but he knew that it would have been futile. He was used to operating on a "need to know" basis, and what his employers generally felt he needed to know was nothing at all. It was perfectly normal for him to be kept in the dark, and there was no use resenting the fact. But he *did* resent it.

He went to the window and looked out over the car-park. He saw Croupion and Carol get into a big black BMW with a yellow Hertz sticker in the corner of the rear windscreen. Belatedly, he began to wish that he had not allowed the thought of dealing with Tommy Ferris to put him off. An Interpol investigation was probably the most exciting thing which would happen all year.

So far, he thought, *this has been an absolute bitch of a day.*

Absurdly mindful of Ramsbottom's ears, he tiptoed back to his desk. Mercifully, the floors were solid enough to keep his conversations one hundred per cent confidential, and he supposed that had to count as a blessing. He settled back in his chair and unfolded his copy of *The Guardian,* deeply grateful that he had no appointments before lunchtime.

* * *

Simon had hardly finished page one when his phone rang. He picked it up with some trepidation, still thinking about the wretched Ramsbottom. But the voice he heard was a booming baritone.

"Sweetland? Tarquin here. I wonder if you could pop over to External Relations for a moment. Got some chaps here from Interpol, no less. Seem to think you might be able to help them." The voice somehow managed to imply that such a possibility lay far beyond the bounds of plausible imagination. Roland Tarquin, Simon knew, was the Birmingham-based Deputy Director of the entire Midlands Division; he had never met the man and felt slightly needled by the tone of contemptuous familiarity.

"That's okay," said Simon, languidly exercising the noble art of one-upmanship, "I've just been chatting with Inspector Croupion. Carol and I were able to steer him in the right direction. Everything's under control."

There was a momentary silence at the other end, then the dull sound of a hand being placed over the mouthpiece. He heard the deputy director speak to someone nearby, but couldn't hear what was said. Then the phone went dead. He shrugged his shoulders, replaced his own receiver and picked up the newspaper again.

He was just turning over to page two when the door of his office opened explosively, and two excessively athletic men hurtled in, diving to either side of the door as they did so. Their arms were extended stiffly before them, and in their hands they held automatic pistols.

"Holy shit!" said Simon, dropping *The Guardian* on the floor. He had not intended to say the words aloud, but they echoed ominously from the walls.

Slowly, the two men lowered their guns and raised themselves from the threatening crouches which they had reflexively assumed. They seemed disappointed, and faintly disgusted.

"It's all clear sir!" one of them called out.

After a moment's pause two other men came in. One was short and tubby, and had to be Roland Tarquin. The other was tall and broad and looked as if he could bend iron bars with his teeth. "Where is he?" asked the big man, shortly. He spoke with a faint accent, which seemed to Simon to be German. Simon nearly said "Who?" but he overcame the reflex, realising that the answer was obvious. He felt a sudden desperate desire not to look like a fool.

"He's gone," he said. "About twenty-five minutes ago. Is something wrong?"

Roland Tarquin looked up at the ceiling, rolled his eyes, and groaned theatrically.

"Describe him," commanded the tall man.

Simon knew by now that he had done something terribly wrong, and struggled to make amends. "Er . . . average height and build," he stuttered, trying desperately to remember. "Very noticeable French accent . . . apart from that, rather . . . well, *very* ordinary."

The tall man muttered something that sounded like *strunz*. "Chameleon," he said, to one of the gunmen.

"Dr Sweetland spends his entire life testing for Talents," said the deputy director, sarcastically. "You can't expect him to detect one when he isn't carrying his Zener cards."

Simon thought that was terribly unfair. The whole point about human chameleons was that they blended in—appearance-wise, at least.

"He was wearing a gaberdine raincoat" he said. "*That* won't blend in terribly well with the mid-day shopping crowd. And he's driving a black BMW with a Hertz sticker in the rear window."

The tall man raised a half-respectful eyebrow. "Licence number?" he asked, hopefully.

"Didn't notice," Simon admitted. "But you can probably get it from Hertz. He's gone to see one of our testees—Tommy Ferris. I take it that he *isn't* from Interpol."

"You take it right, Dr Sweetland," said Tarquin, while the tall man gestured to one of his henchmen. The henchman exited, presumably to call Hertz. The tall man turned back, opening his mouth to ask another question, but Tarquin was by now in full theatrical flow: "You said that you have been—*chatting* was the word, wasn't it?—with this impostor, and that you *steered him in the right direction?*" He seemed to be laying down the groundwork for a full-blown scapegoating exercise.

"He showed me his ID," Simon protested.

The tall man produced an ID card of his own. The photograph was not a good likeness. It identified him as Commander Dieter Lenz. "Like this?" he asked.

"Pretty much," said Simon.

"Did you make any attempt to verify it?"

"No. How was I supposed to do that?"

"I suppose, Dr Sweetland," said Tarquin, nastily, "that it didn't occur to you that an *authentic* Interpol agent would go through the proper channels instead of approaching you directly."

"Actually," said Simon, defensively, "no."

The Director opened his mouth to speak again, but Lenz held up his hand. "Never mind that," he said. "French accent, you say? Genuine, do you think?"

"It sounded genuine," said Simon, suddenly wondering whether it had been just a little too much like a caricature.

"Probably Union Corse," said Lenz, speaking to the remaining gun-man, who had come forward to stand beside him.

"Or some mafioso who thinks it's witty to *pretend* to be Union Corse," said the gunman. "Or maybe a hitman for the gnomes."

Simon stared at them, wondering if he had somehow strayed on to the set of a surreal comedy film.

"What exactly did you tell him?" asked Lenz. "And what's the address he went to?"

"I told him that *sujet Ash*—I mean subject H—was Tommy Ferris. He went to see Tommy, and Carol went with him to act as chaperone."

Lenz looked completely blank. "Subject H?" he repeated, uncomprehendingly.

"That's right. In 'Sortilege and Serendipity'—our paper."

"What the hell are sortilege and serendipity?" demanded Tarquin, with unreasonable asperity. The deputy director was evidently not academically-minded.

"They're the names that British parapsychologists have given to two different sorts of Talent," Simon explained. "Sortilege is the class of Talents which involve finding things by some kind of direct association of ideas or goal-orientated searching; serendipitous Talents are more perverse—people gifted with serendipity can can only find things when they're not actually looking for them."

"And you have written a paper on this subject?" asked Lenz.

"That's right. We presented it in Paris a couple of weeks ago, at the EEC Symposium."

"And subject H?"

"That was one of the case-studies we cited. Tommy Ferris. He has this knack for locating people who've used telephones. Put a receiver in his hand and give him map, and he's dynamite—provided that the phone and the person he's trying to locate are within seven miles of his home, give or take a few hundred yards."

While he was speaking, Simon saw looks of comprehension dawn on the four grim faces arrayed before him. "You *publish* these things?" said the gunman, incredulously. "You shout them from the top of the Eiffel tower? Are you mad?"

Lenz gestured impatiently. "*We* should have known this," he said. "We should not have had to rely on good luck—and it *was* good luck, was it not? When I asked your Director and his Mission Controllers whether any of the Temps on your books could help us, they spent fully half an hour making ridiculous suggestions. If it had not been for that stupid secretary coming in with some irrelevant message about your expenses it would never have occurred to me to wonder whether your expertise as a Tester might be worth consulting. We may have missed this enemy agent, but we must count ourselves lucky that we discovered his existence at all—what was that word again? The word you used to describe such coincidences?"

"Serendipity," said Simon, dully. It had just dawned on him that Carol might be in danger. The man she was with was not an Interpol agent at all, and whatever he was, he was the kind of people that real Interpol agents went after with their guns at the ready.

"We may yet be able to trap him," said Lenz. "The address, please, to which he has gone."

"I can call in the local police," said Tarquin, helpfully, while Simon tapped the keyboard of his desktop terminal, instructing it to call up the Ferris file.

"No," said Lenz, quickly. "The man is too dangerous, and the matter is too delicate. Special Branch only may be involved, and only on a 'need to know' basis."

Simon sighed with relief as the computer displayed Tommy Ferris's record. The system had been remarkably well-behaved of late, since the loathsome Ramsbottom had condescended to lend his expertise to the removal of some awkward bugs.

"13 Corporation Road," he said. "I'll come with you. I know where it is."

"No," said Lenz. "You stay here. I mean *here*. This office." He had already turned on his heel, and his remaining henchman hurried too open the door for him.

"But . . . " Simon began.

"No buts, Sweetland," said Tarquin, acidly, remaining where he was while Lenz and his two companions left. "If this operation goes awry, I want you here for ritual disembowelling." The voice rose in volume as the three men departed, but once they were out of earshot it sank again to a whisper. "You'd better pray that your stupidity doesn't land me in hot water, Sweetland," the deputy director said, leaning forward to make his point. "If there's any comeback on this, from London or Brussels, *your* neck is the one that's going to be on the chopping block. Savvy?"

"But . . . " Simon began again.

"No buts," the Director repeated. "You can consider yourself under office arrest until further notice." And with that, he turned on his heel and marched out.

Simon knew that there was no use trying to demand an explanation. Even if the deputy director knew what was going on, he certainly wouldn't pass on the information. The fact that he would never even be told why his career had gone down the toilet, if indeed that was to be the outcome of his innocent mistake, added an abundance of insult to the probability of injury. For the moment, his resentment of Roland Tarquin even outweighed his resentment of the appalling Ramsbottom.

It was not merely a bitch of day, he decided, but an absolute double-dyed bugger of a day—possibly the worst in his entire life. And it wasn't even half past eleven yet.

Staggered by shellshock, and for want of something better to do, he picked up his newspaper. He tried to resume where he'd left off, but his heart simply wasn't in it. He speculated furiously, instead, as to what could possibly be in Coventry that would interest not only Interpol but also the Union Corse—whoever *they* were—and the mafia. It was obviously something that involved making telephone calls, to *trigger* something . . . and it was apparently something that was important enough to make gnomes hire a hitman . . .

His mind slowly boggled, in its own quiet and relatively dignified fashion.

Then the phone rang again, and when he picked it up his confusion rapidly increased by several more orders of magnitude.

"Monsieur Sweetland," said a soft, accented voice which somehow sounded almost reverent. "Are you playing games wiz me?"

"Certainly," said Simon, bitterly. "Playing games with fake Interpol operatives is my favourite hobby." It was not until he had said it that he realised, uncomfortably, that the powers that be might think it very undiplomatic of him to let Croupion know that he had been rumbled. For a moment, he felt guilty, but only for a moment. *If they keep me in the dark,* he thought, *they can't expect me to produce the right answers off the cuff.*

"I 'ave to 'and it to you," said Croupion, wonderingly. "You are ze coolest customer I 'ave ever dealt with. Eizer zat, or ze craziest. Why did you no' place an ad in ze *Times*, hein? Why do you lay down zis silly patchwork of clues? I admit it, I am ver' confused. But now we know one anozer, oui? You want me to make you an offer, n'est-ce pas?"

Simon stared at the receiver, utterly bewildered. "What kind of offer?" he said, because he simply did not know what else to say.

"Your assistant, she is ver' surprised," the voice continued. "Eizer she is great actress, or she 'ad no idea what *sujet* Ash would tell me. She says she is not your accomplice, and I am inclined to believe her . . . but I must keep her wiz me, must I not? Until we can meet, and settle zis matter. I do not understand zis game we are playing, mon ami, but we are ver' reasonable men. We can give you ze protection you need, and anyzing you desire. Zat is what you want, no?"

It dawned on Simon, slowly and painfully, that Tommy Ferris must have told Croupion that he, Simon, was the person that Croupion was trying to identify. It was just the kind of stroke the little bastard would pull. The idea of feeding duff information to a person with a funny accent was exactly the sort of thing that would tickle his fancy, and the idea of fingering Simon Sweetland must have seemed absolutely perfect to the brat. If Carol had tried to explain, the man who wasn't from Interpol had obviously not believed her.

But what on earth was it, Simon wondered, that Croupion thought that he had done? Exactly what sort of skulduggery was involved here? How much trouble was he in? Ought he to try to explain that Tommy was just playing silly buggers, or what?

He decided to play it cool—or, at any rate, as cool as he could. "Who, exactly, is *we?*" he asked, warily.

"Who do you zink?" countered Croupion, equally warily.

Simon studied the cracks in his office ceiling, considered the situation as carefully as he was able, then shrugged his shoulders and thought *what the hell.* "I figure that you're probably Union Corse," he said, casually. "Unless you're mafia putting on a funny accent to confuse us all. Or maybe—just maybe—you're a hitman for the gnomes."

Croupion laughed. "So you *do* know the score, Monsieur Sweetland—or should I say, *Monsieur Taxman.* Don't worry, mon ami, we always prefer talking to shooting. You 'ave made your point, I zink. Say ze word, an' you are on our team. You must tell me where ze money is, of course . . . a matter of good faith, comprenez? An' you must tell me jus' what your Talent *is* . . . but then everyzing will be on ze table. You only 'ave to name your terms."

"Where exactly are you?" Simon asked, trying to sound casually confident, like a man in complete control of his destiny. "We have to discuss this face to face . . . man to man. Do you want to come back here?"

"I don't zink so," said the man whose name was presumably not

Croupion at all. "I zink you better come to me, hein? I will meet you in ze Cazedral, if you please. Madame Cloxeter and Tommy will be not with me, so we can 'ave a cosy chat. But if anyzing should go wrong . . . I must 'ave a little insurance, comprenez? If anyzing should happen to me . . . somezing also will happen to zem. We are men of ze world, are we not? We understand zese things?"

It was on the tip of Simon's tongue to blurt out a confession of his complete and utter *lack* of understanding, but he kept himself in check. It was far too late for that.

"I'll be there," he promised.

He waited to hear the click at the other end before he put his own receiver down. Only then did he permit himself the luxury of panicking at the thought of what he had done.

His first impulse, on realising that he had thrown himself in at the deep end without knowing whether or not he could swim, was to call the deputy director and ask how he could get in touch with Lenz, but he quashed it. It wasn't so much the thought that if Lenz and his friends showed up at the Cathedral Croupion would simply fade into the background and might then carry out the threat he had made against Carol, though that was certainly an uncomfortable thought; it was more his resentment of the fact that everyone had been, and still remained, so absolutely determined not to tell him what was going on. He wanted desperately to find out what he'd got caught up in, and he felt that whatever happened from now until midnight, the day couldn't possibly get any worse than it already was.

And when I have found out, he thought, *I'll kill that little bastard Tommy Ferris. I'll teach the little sod not to play his stupid practical jokes on* me.

* * *

Simon had never liked Coventry Cathedral. In fact, he didn't like cathedrals in general. They seemed to him to reek of the Middle Ages: of the burning of witches and the vile sanctity of tyranny. Nor were they particularly convenient as meeting-places. Easy to locate they might be, but once inside there were too many little coverts and too many stone pillars. He wandered round for several minutes, wishing that he had at least the glimmer of a talent for sortilege, knowing that he had no chance whatsoever of recognising Croupion's face. After ten minutes of expecting a tap on the shoulder, however, he spotted a gaberdine raincoat in a quiet side-chapel.

The chameleon was slumped quietly in one of the stalls in which the landed gentry had once been privileged to sit. At first, Simon thought that the Frenchman had simply become tired of waiting and had closed his eyes for a moment, but as soon as he touched the shoulder of the gaberdine raincoat he knew that what was beneath it was inert.

Somebody tapped him gently on the back of the neck with something cold and hard and metallic. He had no trouble at all deducing that it must be a gun.

"Lenz?" he said, hopefully.

"Not so loud," whispered a cultured voice, with just the hint of an accent. Simon couldn't quite place it—it wasn't Italian or French, although it just might have been German. Could this, he wondered, be the hitman for the gnomes?

He turned around slowly. The man threatening him with the pistol was not one of Lenz's men, nor was he a chameleon. He was slender, blond and outrageously handsome.

"He's not dead," said the man with the gun, reaching into Simon's inside jacket pocket in order to remove his wallet. "Just sleeping. I probably hit him a bit too hard, but one has to be careful." Simon waited patiently while his Access card, his Switch card, his DPR ID card, his public library borrower's card and his organ-donor's card were carefully inspected. He hoped that he wasn't going to need the last one in the near future.

"A DPR scientist," mused the blond man. "It makes sense, I suppose, that the Taxman would hold some such post. Do you work solo, or have you a little team of Talents at your disposal?"

"I have a team of Talents," Simon said. "Kids mostly, but top class. A lot of kids have raw Talent in abundance, but they don't have the brains to apply it, so they need a Fagin-figure like me. They're very protective too. Every word we say is being monitored, and I've got PKs with power enough to make you eat that gun. I only pass the duds on to the Temp register, you see—I keep all the best ones for my own private practice, as the Taxman."

He rather enjoyed spinning out the fantasy. Although he was making it up as he went along it sounded like a really good idea. He wondered why he'd never thought of doing something of the sort. Probably because kids with Talent were mostly a bunch of delinquent no-hopers, like Tommy Ferris.

The blond man put his gun away, and looked at Simon quizzically.

"Very good, Dr Sweetland," he murmured. "But we live in a world of competing philosophies. Some organizations send out chameleons to do their dirty work, others send out martial arts experts . . . and others send out lie-detectors."

"Ah," said Simon, feeling slightly foolish.

"Bruno Wyss," said the other, holding out his hand to be shaken. "At least, that's what it says on my passport. Wyss with a y, not an ei. After the writer, you know."

Simon inclined his head towards the unconscious Croupion. "I suppose you wouldn't care to tell me who he really is?" he asked, hopefully.

"He's pretending to be mafia pretending to be Union Corse," said Wyss, sitting down in the stall behind Croupion and gesturing an invitation to Simon to join him. "Actually, it's a double bluff. He really *is* Union Corse."

"Exactly what *is* the Union Corse?" asked Simon.

Wyss clucked his tongue. "You really are out of your depth, Dr Sweetland. The Union Corse is a semi-mythical organization, much like the mafia, which runs all the rackets in the south of France. They supposedly originated in Corsica and now base most of their operations in Marseilles."

"Semi-mythical?" Simon queried.

Wyss smiled. He had perfect pearly-white teeth. "Every petty bully-boy from Perpignan to Monaco claims to belong to it in order to make himself seem more dangerous. Because of that, the real members can claim that it's only a legend. But it isn't, as our friend the Taxman clearly knows."

"You don't happen to know where Carol is, I suppose?" said Simon. "Carol Cloxeter—my assistant. He . . . sort of kidnapped her. There's a boy with her—I suppose we'd better rescue him too, if we can."

"All in good time," said Wyss. "But I thought sortilege was supposed to be *your* strong point. Isn't that why our friend sought you out? I was following him, as you must have guessed. Such a pity that chameleons can't make their clothes blend in as readily as their faces, isn't it? What exactly are you doing here, Dr Sweetland? Didn't he get enough information from you when he called at your office?"

Simon had met lie-detectors before, and knew that the best way to deal with them was steadfastly to ignore their questions. "Actually, sortilege is just a sideline," he said, conversationally. "I only got into it because I got into a bit of trouble with my *last* line of research. Anyway, I just try to make up theories about it. I can't actually *do* it. I thought I couldn't do serendipity either, but serendipity is one of those Cinderella Talents that people don't necessarily notice. Two hours ago, I was of the opinion that today's big drama would be losing out on my expenses, but now I seem to have discovered something much more exciting. You *are* the hitman for the gnomes, aren't you, Mr Wyss?"

"That's not the way we do business in Zürich, Dr Sweetland," Wyss told him, his blue eyes radiating injured innocence. "We treat all our customers with respect—even the Union Corse. I have not the slight interest in eliminating the Taxman. Whether he's Talented, or merely talented, he has skills which might be invaluable to us. The best poachers always make the best gamekeepers."

Simon had to remind himself sternly that however personable and amiable Wyss might be, his was not the side of the angels. Dieter Lenz and the men from Interpol were the guys with the badges—but that old cat-killer, curiosity, was still clawing away inside.

"How much has the Taxman managed to rip off?" he asked.

"It's not the quantity," Wyss told him, sternly, "it's the principle. We're supposed to offer total security. Absolute confidence is necessary in our kind of work. It was different in the days when money was yellow metal locked away in iron-clad vaults, ever-ready to be weighed and counted. Now it's just data—numbers which change constantly, and move around the world in the blink of an eye—the electronic vaults which protect it have to be stronger by far than those old iron-clad monsters. Anyone who can get into our vaults threatens the entire system of world finance, and it doesn't really matter whether he fancies himself as some kind of Robin Hood, stealing from organized criminals and leaving his calling card behind—he has to be stopped. We have to get the money back, and we have to find out how he took it, and we have to make sure that no one else gets in the same way."

Simon mentally collated this information with the other hints he had already picked up. "Your thief uses some kind of computer programme—like a virus," he said. "You don't know how he gets it into the system, but you know when it's activated. So you were able to find out that the trigger signal came from Coventry."

"From the central library, to be exact," said Wyss. "The real trouble is that we can't figure out where the money *went*. Arranging a transfer is one thing—finding an undetectable hole in which to stash millions is quite another. We really need to know how his clever little programme managed that."

Simon was still working things out in his head. "You must have traced at least three calls," he said. "That's how Croupion was able to get Tommy to sort out the particular caller he wanted from all the others. Unfortunately, Tommy took it into his head to play one of his little jokes, and landed himself—not to mention Carol and me—in deep trouble. Croupion had already checked my ID, exactly as you did—he'd seen my library card, and that had planted the seed which allowed him to believe Tommy's lie." He stopped abruptly, remembering what he'd scrupulously reminded himself not to do.

"So *that's* why you're here," said Wyss, in a satisfied tone. "Poor Croupion! So, if we can lay our hands on your small friend, and ask him who *really* made the calls, he can tell us. Fortunately, he won't be able to tell *me* any lies."

Simon cursed silently, but not because of what he'd already given away. He felt a sick sensation gripping his stomach. He realised what safety there had been in ignorance, because he also realised that he was no longer ignorant. Now, for the first time, he had a secret to keep—and he was sitting beside a lie-detector who, for all his affability and willingness to chat, was probably not a very nice man.

Wyss moved as if to leave, but hesitated. He regarded Simon contemplatively, as if wondering whether to take him along or leave him behind in the same sorry state as Croupion.

"Why do you call him the Taxman?" Simon asked, hoping to gain time to think and consider his own options.

"It's the calling card he leaves," said the man from Zürich, absent-mindedly. "Whenever he's moved the money out of an account, our machines—and the customer's—print out a statement which declares the account empty and bears, in ludicrously large letters, the words: YOU HAVE JUST BEEN VISITED BY THE TAXMAN."

"And you don't actually know whether he's using some kind of Talent, or whether he's just an expert hacker?"

"Talents always seem to lag a little behind the times," said Wyss, philosophically. "But they catch up, don't they? Now we have computers, those people who have a Talent for messing them up will start to discover the fact. How many people, do you suppose, have lived and died without ever finding out what their Talent was simply because the scope for exercising it wasn't yet there?" While he spoke he leaned forward and started rummaging through Croupion's pockets. Simon guessed that he was looking for the keys to the BMW, which was illicitly parked in a reserved space just outside the cathedral. He wondered whether he dared make a grab for the gun, and decided that he didn't.

"Carol Cloxeter thinks that everybody's Talented," Simon told him. "She thinks consciousness itself is a paranormal phenomenon. She thinks the things we call Talents are just idiosyncratic glitches and trivial side-effects of a miraculous process that we simply take for granted. She thinks that the natural process of mental evolution will eventually give all our children's children competent powers of telepathy and psychokinesis."

"And sortilege," added Wyss, as he discovered the keys in the unconscious man's trousers. "Don't forget sortilege and serendipity."

"If we all had that," Simon said, thoughtfully, "We'd never lose anything, would we? You'd know where all this stolen money had been moved to—we'd all know."

"And we'd be able to find the Taxman just by wondering where he was," Wyss agreed, standing up to go. "A dull world, don't you think?"

In front of them, Jean Croupion suddenly shifted his position and groaned. The rifling of his pockets had obviously jarred him back to the edge of consciousness.

Wyss seemed momentarily uncertain what to do, but then he took out a second pistol from the pocket of his jacket and handed it to Simon. Simon accepted it, wide-eyed with astonishment. "Lest you become confused or over-optimistic," Wyss said, his whisper becoming even more conspiratorial, "the one you've got is the one I took off *him*, and carefully unloaded. The one I have *is* loaded." With that parting shot, he slipped out of the stall and moved stealthily into the shadows, leaving Simon face to face with the awakening racketeer.

Simon had only a second or two to think before Croupion fully recovered consciousness, and he spent the time as best he could. By now, thanks to a fortuitous convergence of sortilege and serendipity, he had found out almost everything. He knew who Wyss was and who Croupion was. He could make a very good guess as to where Carol and Tommy were.

Most important of all, he knew who the Taxman was. There was a slight possibility that Dieter Lenz didn't yet know where he and Croupion were, but it was only slight. Even Special Branch, unaided by any particular Talent, ought to be able to locate a car that was parked outside the cathedral.

Croupion looked up at him distastefully. As he raised himself up and straightened the collar of his raincoat the agent of the Union Corse said: "You didn't have to 'it me, mon ami. I really wasn't going to kill you."

"Maybe," said Simon. "But when you work for the Union Corse, you have to expect that people will be a little reluctant to trust you."

"It really doesn't make any difference zat you 'ave ze gun," said Croupion, probably speaking more truly than he knew. "You wanted to be found, n'est-ce pas? You knew zat sooner or later you would 'ave to talk to *someone*."

"Where's Carol?"

"Who cares? Where is ze money?—zat is what matters."

"You're wrong," Simon told him. "I don't give a damn about the money. The money is irrelevant. But I care about Carol." It was true—every word. The thought that Wyss, if he were still around, would *know* it was true somehow made him feel proud, though he wasn't sure exactly why.

Croupion was studying him carefully, and Simon felt uncomfortable under the speculative gaze. "You really 'ave me confused," the gangster confessed. "But I don' zink you will shoot." And with that, he simply reached out and took the gun out of Simon's hand.

Simon, not knowing what else to do, let him take it.

"I, on ze ozer 'and," said Croupion, "am perfectly 'appy to blow you away. In fact, zat is my intention, if we cannot reach a more amicable settlement."

As Simon looked down the barrel of the unloaded gun, he felt paradoxically brave. He felt as though he were *in control*. Jean Croupion might be one hundred per cent weasel, but the man he was dealing with was not, in his present state of mind, a wimp.

"Carol's locked in the boot of your car, isn't she?" he said, calmly. "Tommy too. You didn't have anywhere else to put them, did you?"

"It's a little cramped," admitted the Frenchman, "but zey'll be perfectly all right, even when you and I take ze ride which we must take. You will *drive* carefully, won't you Monsieur Taxman. You don't want to give your friends a bumpy ride."

"We're not going anywhere," Simon told him. "When I spoke to you on the phone before, I neglected to mention that a posse of real Interpol operatives turned up at my office just after you left. They missed you, but I gave them a description of the BMW. Special Branch have had two hours to find it and stake it out. They'll be waiting patiently for us, outside. Being a chameleon, you *might* just slip through the net—but not if you have me with you." Raising his voice, he added: "And the same goes for you, Mr. Wyss." He wasn't absolutely sure that Wyss was still listening, but he knew that all lie-detectors were inveterate eavesdroppers.

Croupion looked round, confusion turning to resentment.

Bruno Wyss stepped out of the shadows. He didn't have a gun in his hand.

"You and I are on the same side, Monsieur Croupion," he said, softly. "We both want the same things: the money returned, the Taxman put out of action."

Croupion didn't react immediately, but he must have decided that it was true.

"Well," he said, viciously, "at least we can take care of ze last item."

He brought the gun up to Simon's forehead, and without the least delay or ceremony, pressed the trigger.

Even though he had every reason to believe that the gun really was un-loaded, Simon felt his heart lurch and his bowels quiver—but he didn't faint, or suffer any more embarrassing fate, because the silent scream of fear which echoed through his being was drowned by the tide of elation which followed the harmless clicking of the trigger.

Wyss shrugged his shoulders. "Sorry, mon ami," he said—addressing Croupion rather than Simon—"but as the English like to put it, discretion really is the better part of valour. Anyhow, Dr Sweetland is not the Taxman. You found the wrong man."

Croupion frowned. "But ze boy . . . " he began. Simon was able to watch comprehension dawn in the man's unguarded features, and knew that Croupion had duplicated his own deduction.

He had only a split second in which to act, and he knew that now he *had* to act. Had he been a policeman, or a racketeer, or a film actor, he would probably have been able to move with smooth swift grace to fell Bruno Wyss with a perfect right hook, but knowing his limitations as he did, he simply put his head down and ran full tilt at the blond man, intending to head-butt him squarely in the chest.

His head made painful if muffled contact with the gun in Wyss's shoulder-holster. The blond man let out a howl of outrage, and went down like a skittle. Simon ran straight over him, careless of any damage which his size nine black oxfords might do to the other's outrageous handsomeness.

Somewhere behind him Simon heard Croupion say: "*Merde!*" in a half-respectful fashion that was music to his ears. Then he started yelling, at the top of his voice: "Lenz! Lenz! Get the guy in the gaberdine and the blond guy with the gun!"

Mercifully, this plea did not fall on deaf ears. With or without the aid of supernatural sortilege, Special Branch *had* found the car. Pretty soon, Simon knew, *everyone* would have figured who the Taxman was—except, perhaps, for Bruno-the-Lie-Detector Wyss.

* * *

In the confusion which reigned while the men from Interpol and Special Branch overcame the heroic but ultimately ineffectual resistance put up by Croupion and Wyss, Simon had no difficulty in making his way to his own car. He felt slightly guilty about not racing to the side of his newly-liberated assistant, but just at that moment the one thing he wanted more than anything else in the world was to be the first person to confront the master-criminal who had ripped off millions from the most secret and most secure bank-accounts in all the world.

Marcia was still out to lunch when he got back to the DPR, and the corridors of the annexe were deserted. When Simon entered the office directly beneath his own, Ramsbottom looked up disinterestedly from the screen into which he had been peering. The green glow reflected from his cheeks made him look like something three-quarters dead.

"Dr Sweetland," he said, colourlessly. "How can I help you?"

Simon sat down in the familiar rock-hard chair which Ramsbottom kept for his interrogatees. "I've got a query about my expenses," he said, his voice dripping with resolute sarcasm.

"Indeed?" said Ramsbottom, quite unembarrassed. "I thought that we had settled the matter to our mutual satisfaction."

"What I want to know," said Simon, grimly, "is how the hell you have the brass neck to exert every fibre of your scrawny being to the task of screwing me out of a lousy five hundred francs, when you spend your spare time—and, at a guess, a substantial fraction of the DPR's time—stealing millions of francs, deutschemarks, pounds, dollars and every other currency under the sun from numbered Swiss bank accounts operated by the mafia and the Union Corse? And also how you have the nerve to add insult to injury by proclaiming in your own uniquely mealy-mouthed fashion that screwing me out of my expenses is a matter of bloody *principle?*"

Ramsbottom leaned back slightly in his chair, slightly reducing the greenness of his gills. Simon had hoped to see signs of guilt, alarm, astonishment and disappointment, but there were none in evidence.

"Ah," said the accountant, neutrally.

"Ah!" Simon repeated, injecting as much outrage and disgust into the expostulation as the lone syllable was capable of carrying. "Is that all you can say? Ah! Some slimy French gangster just shoved a gun in my face and tried to blow my bloody head off, under the mistaken impression that I was you, and all you can say is *ah!* Jesus, Ramsbottom, for two pins I'd kick you all the way from here to bloody Wolverhampton."

"I assumed that I would be found out eventually, of course," observed Ramsbottom, with just the slightest hint of wonderment in his tone, "but I must confess that I had never imagined that you would be the one to do it, Dr Sweetland."

"Well," said Simon, "I *was* the one to do it. It was pure serendipity, but I did it. We only have about thirty minutes before the world and his wife catches up with me, but I just wanted you to know that I was the first. And I wanted to ask you my question—which you seem to be ignoring."

Ramsbottom nodded slowly. "Well," he said, lugubriously, "I suppose I owe you that much. But as a matter of interest how, exactly, *did* you find out?"

"Tommy Ferris fingered you," said Simon, curtly. "He was one of our case-studies. He's a kid who can identify the current whereabouts of people who've used telephone receivers—as you would undoubtedly know if you had bothered to *read* our paper instead of just ripping off our fee. When the people who were trying to track you down traced the source of the calls you were making to trigger your clever electronic thieves, one of them was bright enough to realise that Tommy could locate you. The kid was bang on the button—but he located you on a two-dimensional street map. When he pointed to the vital spot, nobly suppressing his practical joking tendencies because he was under the mistaken impression that he was helping Interpol, the guy who had been in my office less than an hour before, and had already clocked my library card, promptly jumped to the wrong conclusion. And when the poor puzzled fellow phoned me in order to confirm his suspicions I contrived, for entirely the wrong reasons, to put the final touches to his delusion. At that point, I still hadn't a clue what was going on, but when the gnomes' hitman kindly enlightened me, I was finally able to put two and two together and come up with a Ramsbottom."

"Ah," said Ramsbottom.

"Why?" said Simon, as softly as he could. "Just tell me why?"

"I'm not sure you'd understand," said Ramsbottom, with a strange reedy sigh. "On the other hand, maybe you see it every day of the week, in all those kids you test. Perhaps they all want to be superheroes. Perhaps every single one of them wants, more fervently than anything else in the world, to be the next Sharkman or the new Lady Wolverene, or Kid Spectrum the Second, or Son of Dr Miraculous. Maybe *everyone* has the same dream, deep down—the dream which says, 'What you see isn't the *real* me. It's just a sham, a charade. Inside, my *secret* identity is a million times better, a million times stronger, a million times more enviable.' They don't ever tell you that, though, do they, Dr Sweetland? Even kids have to learn to suppress their dreams. They learn that if they say it out loud, people will mock—mock them for not being Talented, or mock them because the Talents they do have are so stupid, so useless, so inadequate. They learn that they have to be ordinary and despicable in other people's eyes."

Ramsbottom's voice suddenly hardened. " But *inside*, Dr Sweetland," he said, bitterly, "it's different. Inside, they're men of steel. They're caped crusaders or hooded avengers, fighting to keep the world safe for justice and democracy. I wonder if you do understand, Dr Sweetland. I wonder if even *you* feel like that deep down. Maybe, like me, you've felt that way ever since you realised that bullets wouldn't bounce off you, that you'd never be able to fly, and that you don't have X-ray eyes. How do you *feel*, Dr Sweetland, as you do your job, day in and day out—as you process all those kids, and smash all their dreams?"

Simon blinked when Ramsbottom paused, but he couldn't find anything to say. This wasn't what he'd expected.

"Do you know how people loathe and despise me, Dr Sweetland?" asked Ramsbottom, rhetorically. "Of course you do. You understand completely. But it never occurred to you to wonder, did it, how I might feel about that? I have no Talent, Dr Sweetland—-no Talent at all. At least, I didn't have, until the DPR kindly gave me *these*." He spread his arms wide to indicate his rampart of screens. "I spent years learning to use these things, finding out what they can do. I don't think there's anything paranormal about my affinity for them, but it doesn't really matter, in the end, whether you get your results by clicking your magic fingers or by sheer hard graft, as long as you get there. I knew, from the moment I made the acquaintance of these machines, that with them I could realise my dreams. I knew that if I worked at it, I could *be* a masked avenger, a man of mystery, a scourge of the Underworld. And I knew, too—because by then I was no longer a little boy seething with violent resentment against the playground bullies, but an *accountant*—that I could do the job *properly.* I'd learned that violence doesn't solve anything, and that it's utterly beside the point whether you rip criminals to shreds with your bare hands, or throw them into overcrowded jails for a hundred years; I knew that the *proper* way to fight cruelty and injustice, the only viable way to make the world honest and good, was to inject some much-needed truth into the finest but least convincing motto in the world: **CRIME DOESN'T PAY.**"

Simon coughed to clear the lump from his throat, impressed in spite of himself. But then he curled his lip, and said: "All very admirable. And I'm sure that the mafia and the Union Corse have got the message. But *your* crimes seem to have paid off pretty well, don't they?"

Ramsbottom shook his head sorrowfully. "Oh, Dr Sweetland," he said, weakly and apparently without an ounce of resentment, "you still don't see it, do you? I didn't *steal* the money. Why do you think that they couldn't work out where it went, even though they have the entire world financial system at their beck and call? I just *deleted* it. I wiped it out. It doesn't exist any more. That's the DPR philosophy, you see. In America, crime-fighting is all fabulous fascists in funny costumes, but we're supposed to be different, aren't we? We're supposed to do things the British way—or, from now on, the *European* way. That's what I've tried to do. No violence; no spectacle; just an educational message, delivered in the only universal language there is: *crime doesn't pay.*"

Simon remembered what Wyss had said about the world having changed. Money wasn't heaps of yellow metal any more. It wasn't solid. It could simply be made to disappear. **YOU HAVE JUST BEEN VISITED BY THE TAXMAN.** Quicker on the draw than the European Parliament; more deadly than the European Court of Human Rights; less bureaucratic than the Common Agricultural Policy: *The Taxman!* The perfect EEC superhero.

Ramsbottom seemed to have shrunk visibly now that he had got it all off his chest. His fervour had exhausted itself, and he was no longer tautly in control of himself. He seemed nervous, now.

In the distance, there was the faint sound of a siren wailing. The people who were coming for Ramsbottom wouldn't be sounding any sirens, of course, but the plaintive whine seemed poignantly symbolic.

"Will they send me to jail, do you think?" asked Ramsbottom, plaintively.

Simon looked around the dingy office, reduced to half its natural size by the ancient banks of dead, dusty files. He looked at the desk which Ramsbottom had carefully rebuilt as a fortress in order to to keep the world at bay. Finally, he looked at the sallow face and the ridiculous moustache of the absurd little man who never went home until the day's work was completely done.

"Yes they will," he said, sadly. "You'll be living in maximum security luxury for the rest of your life. Your every need will be attended to, if not your every whim. You'll have as many terminals to play with as you can possibly use, and all the time in the world. Everyone who speaks to you will be utterly and absolutely respectful, and they'll toast your every accomplishment in vintage champagne. I don't know whether you'll be in London or Paris or Berlin, but wherever you are, you'll be the greatest treasure in the land, helping to make the world safe for democracy, justice and honest money. And every gnome in Zürich will be weeping and gnashing his teeth over the fact that Switzerland isn't a member of the EEC. It's going to be really tough, Ramsbottom, but you'll just have to take it like a man. Like a true-blue through-and-through taxman."

Ramsbottom thought about that for a few seconds, and then he smiled. Perhaps for the first time in his long, arduous and frustrated life, Ramsbottom smiled.

* * *

"I hear that you probably saved my life," said Carol Cloxeter, with just the faintest hint of irony. It was all over, and she had broken the habit of a lifetime by stopping off at his flat for a cup of coffee on the way home.

"Think nothing of it," said Simon. "It was the least I could do. After all, it was me who delivered you into the hands of the evil criminal mastermind, so it was down to me to help you out. It's a pity that nobody but Roland

Tarquin will ever find out what a hero I was. Anyway, Interpol and Special Branch helped a bit. How was Tommy feeling when you took him home?"

"Over the moon. Not only did his Talent identify the most wanted man in Europe but he got to be tied up and left in the boot of a BMW for several hours, and he can proudly declare to all his friends that he's been sworn to absolute secrecy about the true nature of the operation, thus conveniently covering up the fact that he doesn't actually know anything at all. Not bad for a kid whose future once seemed to be limited to fingering phone freaks."

"If I hadn't hated the little brat so much, I might have figured everything out much earlier. It seemed so obvious that he'd dropped me in it. Did you figure out what the true state of play was?"

"I didn't have the chance. I didn't even see where Tommy's finger was pointing—Croupion very carefully blocked my view. I didn't have time to figure out what his stupid questions were getting at before he turned into a human whirlwind and had us both tied up and gagged. You have no idea how uncomfortably it is to lie folded up in the boot of a car, bound and gagged and face to face with an unwashed wriggling child, absolutely bursting to go to the loo. Special Branch got me out just in time. Just my luck to get the damsel-in-distress role. Next time, can I be the one who goes to the secret rendezvous in the cathedral?"

"You wouldn't have liked it," Simon assured her. "It was okay until Croupion put the gun to my head, but my insides didn't quite believe Mr. Wyss's reassurances about it not being loaded. I wouldn't wish that particular moment on anyone, let alone someone I . . . like." He quickly put his coffee-cup to his lips to hide the slip.

She looked at him rather oddly. "I . . . like . . . you too," she said, in a voice which was perfectly even. She didn't need to add the word *but*, or trail off significantly in a line of imaginary dots; he understood the qualification very well. Its name was Edward Cloxeter.

"Well," said Simon, with a sigh, "you might change your mind about that when I tell you what happened this morning. You see, I had to go see the amazing Ramsbottom about our expense-claim for the Paris trip, and . . . "

He explained, apologetically, why Carol wasn't going to get her half of the fee for the publication of "Sortilege and Serendipity".

She took it very well, all things considered. All she said, in the end, was: "I suppose it just goes to prove that no one *ever* gets the better of a real superhero."

SKINNED ALIVE

The Great Scientist drew the curtains over the French windows, and then turned back to his guest. The room seemed much warmer with the cold Autumnal darkness tucked tidily away out of sight. He made his way back to his favourite chair, by the fireside, and sat down. His gaze dwelt briefly on the young reporter's legs. This was no weather, he thought, for walking around in a skirt that left the knees exposed. It was strange how fashions moved—the last time skirts had been so short was half a lifetime away, in the nineteen-sixties. He had been in his early teens then, and the world had seemed very different. He wondered whether wearing the short skirt might be a tactical move on the girl's part, intended to distract him while her shrewd questions penetrated his private thoughts. He had a sneaking suspicion that the editors of *Chic* magazine might be more interested in his private life than in his beloved science. That seemed to be the way of the world nowadays.

But there was no denying that the young reporter had very pretty legs.

Jennifer, meanwhile, was having second thoughts about the wisdom of wearing the short skirt. It wasn't the sort of thing that one supposedly needed to worry about nowadays, but the professor belonged to an older generation, whose attitudes had been formed in the mid-twentieth century, and he was probably too old to adapt to modern times. She guessed that he must be over sixty, and he was already showing signs of decrepitude: thick-lensed spectacles for chronic short sight, and an old-fashioned hearing-aid perched precariously behind his left ear.

Professor Birnam took off his spectacles and polished the lenses assiduously, trying to forget about legs, tight sweaters and the nineteen-sixties. When he replaced them, he found that the girl was smiling. She had a nice smile. He grinned in return, rather nervously.

"Where was I?" he asked.

"You were about to tell me," she said, pleasantly, "exactly how you came by your wonderful idea."

"Pardon?" he said, foolishly.

Jennifer patiently repeated what she had said, trying to enunciate clearly without actually raising her voice. The hearing-aid was working, it was just that the old man was flustered.

"Oh . . . yes . . . the idea. Well, in a manner of speaking, it wasn't exactly *my* idea. Not entirely. It was my wife, you see. She always wanted a fur coat—a *real* fur, you know, not one of the modern synthetics. We couldn't afford one—you know better than most, I suppose, how much an antique fur costs. It began as a kind of ambition, and ended up, ultimately, as something of an obsession. My wife wasn't what you might call an understanding woman. She couldn't understand why I didn't earn much money. She never really had much *feeling* for pure science and the quest for knowledge. She used to say that even if I found it, it wouldn't pay the electricity bills. We . . . er . . . argued a lot. And one day I told her that fur coats didn't grow on trees, and she . . . it was rather a witty reply, actually . . . said: 'Well, if you're the greatest geneticist in the world, why can't you *make* fur coats grow on trees?'

"It was a joke, but . . . well, you get to thinking about these things. It seemed silly, but it kept going round in my mind, and I thought, well . . . why not? It seemed quite an interesting challenge . . . scientifically speaking."

"I think that's simply wonderful," said Jennifer. She usually found on these occasions that it was worth laying on the flattery a bit thick. There was a first-rate story in this, if she could get it right, and she was lucky to have got on to it so quickly. She toyed speculatively with possible headlines: **REAL FUR IS BACK! . . . COATS WITHOUT CRUELTY . . . GENIUS NAGGED BY WIFE INTO INVENTION OF THE CENTURY** . . . she had to get the personal angle in there somehow. She wondered, idly, whether "breakthrough" was better than "invention".

"Basically," said the Great Scientist, speaking just a little hurriedly, "the problem was one of induced local cytogenetic metamorphosis. What we had to do was intrude into the mature cell-mass of the tree a component of alien cells, to act as a stimulant to new growth, ideally leading to the achievement of symbiotic synergistic synthesis between two normally-incompatible tissues.

"The incompatibility of the tissues, of course, has to be overcome by inhibiting the *specific* reactivity of the cell systems, while simultaneously revitalising the more generalised *adaptive* reactivity normally observed in the embryonic induction process. Revitalising induction processes, of course, has been my particular field for many years . . . "

The Great Scientist broke off as he realised that Jennifer was balancing her pencil on her lower lip, and did not seem to be paying attention. "Are you . . . er . . . are you getting all this?" he mumbled.

"Oh yes," said the young reporter brightly. "Perfectly fascinating. But it's not *exactly* the kind of thing I'm after. What our readers want is the human angle. You, of course, tend to see your discovery only in scientific terms, but you will appreciate that to the fashion world it is the beginning of a *revolution*. Since it became illegal to slaughter rare animals in order to make fur coats we've seen some nice new synthetic materials, but it's never been quite the *same* as the old days. As you pointed out, antique furs have become well-nigh priceless. Your discovery could transform the whole situation. By this time next year everyone—everyone, at any rate, who's *in*—will be wearing *your* mink and leopardskin, which are just like the real thing...."

"They are the real thing," said Professor Birnam, just a little rudely. "There's no fakery about this, young lady. The pelts are produced by cells which are actually mink or leopard cells, grafted on to trees in the active layer underlying the bark. Eventually, the bark just peels away, you see, because the revitalised induction process affects the germinal tissue of the cork cambium . . . "

Jennifer, sensing that another long and quite incomprehensible scientific monologue was about to develop, felt that a change of subject was in order.

"What's that noise?" she said, abruptly.

The Great Scientist stopped dead and listened. As he listened, of course, he lost the whole thread of his argument. There was no sound at all, except for the wind rustling the boughs of the ash trees behind the house, but he put up his hand reflexively, as if to fiddle with his hearing-aid, which was nearly dislodged from its position.

The girl smiled again. "Must have been my imagination," she said.

"Now, where were we? Oh yes . . . your experiments were carried out right here in the grounds, weren't they? Your wife must have taken a keen interest in them. Was she a continuing source of . . . inspiration?"

The Great Scientist blinked, and said: "Pardon?"

"Inspiration," said Jennifer. "Your wife."

Professor Birnam gave a creditable imitation of a hollow laugh. "I wouldn't exactly call it inspiration," he said. "She got quite bitter about the whole thing. She seemed to think that I was insulting her in some way . . . being deliberately silly and taking up her sarcastic comment just to make a mockery of of her. I don't think she ever for one moment thought that I was serious. And she obviously never considered the possibility that I might succeed. She really *didn't* understand. Sometimes I think she must have been the least understanding person in the world . . .

"It must have been a great shock to you when she left you."

"Between you and me," said the Great Man, his voice tremulous with nervous confidentiality, "it was a blessed relief. If I'd thought for one minute that the young man I brought in to look after the trees would run off with her I'd have . . . I'd have hired an assistant years ago. Mind you, he wasn't much good with the trees. Couldn't tell an ash from an elm. And he didn't really understand what I was doing any better than *she* did. Kept muttering things about it being unnatural, and swore that no good would come of it. These country folk, you know . . . "

"But in a way," interposed the girl, provocatively, "he had a point. There is something about the notion of crossing a leopard with an ash tree which doesn't seem *quite* natural."

The Great Scientist looked suddenly stern. "You're not one of those people who think that if God had meant mink coats to grow on trees he would have arranged it himself, are you?"

"Oh no," the young reporter assured him, quick to rescue herself. "I think what you've done is *marvellous*. A great boon to humanity. I really do."

The Great Man repented his harshness. "You're a very intelligent young lady," he said, with no more than a hint of awkwardness.

She simpered. She was good at simpering. She practised occasionally. Very few girls these days bothered with the art and science of flirtation but Jennifer felt that it was nice to be able to draw on such resources in time of need. It all helped to develop one's career.

The Great Man was completely overcome. "You understand these things far better than *them*," he said. "I think you're beginning to see the true significance of it all. You must try to realise what it means to *me* . . . the long, desperate struggle . . . and the exhilarating success. At first, you know, I will confess, I had my doubts. Experimental genetics is like . . . oh, like cookery without a recipe book . . . you always know what you're putting in but you're never quite sure what's going to come *out* of it all."

"Certainly sounds like my cooking," said the reporter, *sotto voce*.

The Great Scientist frowned momentarily, obviously not having heard what she said, but he let it pass. "Some of the early effects," he said, "were really quite startling. Random appearance of parenchymatous cell bundles . . . de-differentiation of the tunica . . . even mutational polyploidy in the generating xylem! There were effects in the crown too—rubicund pigmentation in the leaves and increased elasticity in the branches. Positively amazing! It will take years to track all the consequences of the transformation and understand it fully. But the *essential* experiment succeeded magnificently. You have no idea how exciting it was when the bark flaked off and revealed what was underneath. Flawless skins! Superb . . . !"

He was, at this point, so carried away that he leaned forward and reached across to place his hand upon the Young Reporter's knee. She could feel the sweat on his palm through her tights. She coughed delicately, but he didn't even notice. In desperation, she resorted to her standard ploy.

"Now this time," she said, loudly, "I really *did* hear something!"

The Great Man looked toward the curtained windows, startled.

"What?"

He hadn't removed his hand.

"Outside," she improvised. "As if someone was walking about near the trees."

"Oh, nonsense," he said. "Why would anyone be out there? There's nothing to steal, you know. Not now. The last few pelts were harvested last week. They're at the furriers, as you know."

"The *trees* are still valuable, though," she said lamely. Her mind was not on the subject. She was trying desperately to think of another polite stratagem. His clammy hand was horrible, but she couldn't upset the old man. It wouldn't be diplomatic. She tried moving her knee sideways a little.

Professor Birnam suddenly realised where his hand was, and where it had been for some seconds. He snatched it away, guiltily. His face went quite red. In order to cover up his confusion, he babbled out an answer to her comment. "Well, of course . . . the *trees* are . . . er . . . valuable. Next year they'll produce a new crop . . . one of the best things about the process . . . .but no one's going to walk off with a tree, now are they? They're not saplings, you know . . . full grown, healthy ash trees . . . plus a touch of leopard or mink, too, of course."

It all sounded rather inane. Jennifer felt that it was time to steer the discussion toward more promising ground.

"Didn't you feel just terrible," she asked, "harvesting the pelts? I mean, you'd put so much into this work . . . you must have become quite emotionally involved with your trees . . . and then it all ended with their being practically *skinned alive.*"

"Oh no," said the scientist, looking genuinely surprised. "That's most misleading. I hope you won't say that in your article. Trees don't get upset, you know. They don't feel a thing. Very placid temperament, trees."

"But they aren't wholly trees," she said. "Not any more. They're half leopard. Or half mink."

"Oh, by no means," said Birnam, earnestly. "Not *half*. Not even a quarter. Just the layers outside the cambium . . . the outer skin."

"But surely," persisted the reporter, "it's the animal part that was actually *stripped of its skin.* Not the plant part."

The geneticist clicked his tongue. "You mustn't *say* things like that," he said. "You're using emotional terminology. There's no place for emotion in science. I assure you that the harvesting went very smoothly. Nothing cruel about it—no fuss and no bother . . . except, well . . . it did seem that removing the pelts might stimulate further change. The exposed cell layers have been picking up some of that pigment that got into the leaves, and there's been a sort of acceleration of elastic cell-growth in the xylem . . . but there was no *pain*. Nothing like that at all. I thought you *understood* . . . "

"Oh, I do," said Jennifer, soothingly. "I *do*. How long did you say it would take to grow new pelts?"

The old man relaxed again. "A year," he said. "They're shedding their leaves now, of course, with it being Autumn. I'm going to begin experiments with evergreens next year, though—pine, spruce and fir . . . "

The young reporter was feeling rather cramped. She uncrossed her legs and massaged her left calf, then crossed them again. The procedure drew the scientist's gaze like a magnet. Her skirt had ridden up an extra inch or two, and he was staring.

The embarrassment was becoming too much to bear, for both of them. Jennifer felt that it was time to draw matters to a close.

"Would you say, professor," she said, quickly, "that what you've achieved is a great step forward for experimental science as well as a god-send for the fur trade?" She was fishing for a good quote. It sounded a bit lame, but she could always beef it up a bit later, as long as she could get him to agree in principle.

"Oh yes," blurted Professor Birnam. He whipped off his spectacles again, trying to dismiss the feelings of carnal lust welling up inside him, but in the process he dislodged the hearing-aid from his ear. Without his spectacles, he could not see where it fell. In great confusion he began to polish the lenses with his handkerchief, removing imaginary specks of dust with great vigour and determination. "Of course . . . " he said.

Jennifer leaned over to pick up the hearing-aid, and held it out to him, but before he could replace his spectacles and take it from her there was a colossal crash.

The French windows imploded, and through the shattered glass came a hideous creature, branches waving wildly, claws raking the air, blood pouring from every knot-hole. Its fang-filled mouths were *slavering,* and its roots were already beginning to ooze across the Persian carpet.

The Great Scientist peered myopically over his shoulder as an uneasy feeling crept over him that all was not quite as it should be.

"Of course," he went on, bravely, "there might be one or two little snags that we haven't hit yet . . . "

TAKEN FOR A RIDE

As soon as he had finished his evening meal Joe rode the Bakerloo line from Lambeth up to Piccadilly Circus, arriving just in time to take up the fifteen-minute slot he'd booked on the new so-called Virtual Reality machine at the Trocadero. It was a gyroscopically-mounted sensurround that could do full rotations in all three dimensions, giving the rider the impression of a theme park roller-coaster ride even though it was anchored to the spot. The rider was supposed to be strapped in the pilot's seat in an interstellar spaceship, but the game involved zapping spacewhales, voidsharks and cloudcloaks instead of enemy ships firing off implausibly noisy lasers.

Joe enjoyed the session. He had been in far too many flight-simulators to be fooled by the game's special effects and the instructive voice piped into his earphones was unnecessarily strident, but the visuals were good and there was a certain intellectual challenge in figuring out the various kinds of natural defences the wildlife had. He didn't bother worrying about the plausibility or otherwise of nuclear-powered wildlife carrying on the red-clawed struggle for existence in intergalactic dust-clouds—some things you just had to take as given.

He scored just under 33,000. The machine assured him that this was way above average, but Joe the Arcade Ace couldn't be satisfied with that, given that the machine had only been in place a week and the average must have been calculated almost entirely from the scores of debutants. He was sure he could double up next time, now that he'd figured out the elements of the winning strategy.

The game might have been more exciting if he'd been slightly high, but it was Thursday and he was at rock-bottom. He always came down for the working week so as not to take the risk of fouling up in the lab. His work there was time-serving routine with no real bite but he wanted his doctorate badly and he was just as desperate to get a good score on that as he was to master every latest PC challenge. You couldn't get anywhere these days in Industrial Chemistry or Pharmaceuticals unless you had a doctorate with distinction—a common-or-garden BSc was just so much toilet paper. But one of the best things about bumping along at ground zero from Monday nine to Friday five was looking forward to a real orbital boost Friday night, and now was the time to get fixed up. Back in the Underground he hopped on Old Indigo and rode up to King's Cross to make his connection.

Joe enjoyed his trips to King's Cross, all the more so since the police had started their fourteenth crusade to clean up the area. He liked the surreal atmosphere the place had, and the heightened self-consciousness that came from knowing that this square mile had a greater density of hidden spy-cameras than any other in the land, not excepting the Forbidden City itself. The tension began to build while he was still on the tube-train, and when the escalator carried him up into the station it gradually grew into a buzz which was as exhilarating, in its way, as a hit—not as intense or as long-lasting as a fruitcake or a couple of Es, but nice in its own way.

Out of the Underground, into the Underworld, he thought, as he dodged around the well-heeled queue for the Virgin Executive Shuttle to Edinburgh and made his way out of the brilliantly-lit concourse into the neon-stained night. It gave him a big lift to think that he knew his way around this little circle of the Underworld, that he had a reliable supplier who always had authentic MDMA, none of your badly-cooked MDA or LSD-methyl cocktails. He liked walking the *étal,* having the girls call out to him, even though he was never tempted—why pay for a hurried screw in a rubber suit when you could buy the *real thing* just a little way down the line? Joe took pride in being a discerning consumer who spent his fun money wisely.

It was raining when he got out of the station, but that didn't dampen his spirits. The rain seemed somehow *apt,* like the rain that was always falling in certain kinds of *film noir* scenes. He would have had the hood of his anorak up anyway, because of the cameras. The deal itself would be done in the dark, in some briefly-shielded corner where everyone was cosily

131

safe from nightsights, but he always liked to be careful about being spotted going in and out. He was already on file with the drug squad, so it wouldn't make any real difference if they got one more blurred snap for his album, but he didn't want to attract *too much* attention—after all, he had his future career to think about. He wasn't a long-term loser like the fleshwads on the ,tal or the petty pushers; he had his first class honours on the wall and his doctorate in the bag. In the Underworld he was strictly a tourist and an untouchable. He'd never been tempted to overbuy so that he could hawk it around the college, any more than he'd been tempted to start a home-brew project in the labs; that sort of involvement was far too risky.

The crazy thing was that when the two guys grabbed him as he was coming out of the alley, it seemed more like an extra twist to the excitement than a total disaster. It was a bummer, but there was an edge to it, like reaching a level he'd never reached before in a particularly difficult game. He didn't relish the prospect of losing the Es he'd just bought, or taking another caution from the boys in blue, but he wasn't scared and he didn't panic.

"Hey!" he said, to the guy on his right, who seemed positively mountainous in the half-light. "Gently! Didn't you forget to show me a warrant card?"

Neither of them replied, but that didn't bother Joe. He already knew that he had the right to remain silent, etc—and all the crap that went with it. Nor did it bother him that the guys who'd grabbed him weren't in uniform—the DS always looked far worse than the pushers and the pimps. The only real shock he got was when the big man's face was briefly illuminated, and he saw how empty it was: devoid of expression, of personality, of everything.

Whatever he's on, Joe thought, *must be one hell of a dazer.*

Then he saw the vehicle they were taking him to. It was parked on the road, illegally, but no one was complaining. It was a Rolls Royce Silver Shadow. It was at least twenty years old, but that made it all the more impressive—it was the kind of motor whose price went up, not down, with age and its condition was immaculate. Nothing in the world could have looked less like a paddy-wagon. To add injury to insult, the blond guy standing beside it was far too well-dressed to be a cop in drag, and far too cadaverous to be a merchant.

Oh shit! Joe thought. *Wrong place, wrong time, wrong man. Some embarrassment coming up.* He still wasn't scared; he just assumed that it was a case of mistaken identity—that the Incredible Hulk had plonked his mechanical-shovel hands on the wrong target.

Unfortunately, the blond guy didn't make any protest to that effect. He just opened the back door of the Silver Shadow. The Hulk bundled Joe into the back seat, and followed him in. The blond man got into the front passenger seat, directly in front of Joe, while the third one got into the driver's seat.

A little light in the ceiling above Joe's seat flicked on, showing him a wall of glass separating him from the blond man, who immediately turned to scrutinise him.

It was when the blond man showed no indication at all that he was aware of the fact that his bully-boys had picked up the wrong man that Joe finally conceded to himself that he might be in *real* trouble.

* * *

The light thrown out by the tiny bulb was eerily blue, and so much of it reflected back off the glass partition that the face of the blond man seemed ghostly, less clear in Joe's eyes than his own reflection, but Joe could see that the face was thin and very pale except for a curious yellowy tint, old-looking without being wrinkled. The blond hair was groomed to perfection; the dark jacket, white shirt and dark silk tie were equally precise.

If there had been any doubt remaining in Joe's mind as to the fact that this was a very wealthy man the fixtures and fittings in the back of the Rolls would have dispelled it. The outside was 1980s but the inside was very turn-of-the-Millennium, Gadget City in miniature. The only jarring presence was the huge man who sat beside him on the tan leather seat, still and silent—almost as though he had been *switched off.* He wasn't spectacularly ugly, in spite of his porcine physiognomy, but he was utterly androidal. He reminded Joe of a ventriloquist's dummy blown up to ten or twelve times natural size.

"I'm sorry, guys," Joe blurted out, uneasily, "but you have the wrong person. I'm a customer, not a dealer. In any war you've got going, I'm just a civilian."

The driver was the first to speak. He asked the blond man, curtly, if it was all okay.

"Yes," said the blond man, after looking Joe over very carefully. "That's him. Let's go." His voice, muffled by the glass partition, was as ghostly as his face. Joe's stomach felt queasy.

As the driver started the engine Joe tested the door, thinking that there might still be time to bail out and run, if he could just move fast enough to evade the android wrestler—but the door had a child-proof lock which ensured that it could only be opened from the outside.

The driver slid the Rolls into gear and it moved off smoothly. Joe was astonished by how quiet it was inside; the noise of the engine was no more than a purr.

"I'm not a dealer," Joe said, insistently, desperate to get the point across in spite of the partition. "I'm a postgraduate student at Imperial College. Check my wallet—it has my library card in it, with a photo. I'm not whoever you think I am."

"You're Joseph Redmond Rutherford, born 20 September 1979," said the blond man, who was still twisted in his seat, looking back at his prisoner. "There's no mistake, Joe, I assure you of that." His softened voice sounded more pitying than hostile—and that, to Joe, was the most menacing thing of all.

Joe knew that the blond man must be telling the truth about there being no mistake; no one could possibly have found out his middle name without doing some serious research. It was his mother's maiden name, given to him out of some weird sense of propriety, and he never used it—not even on forms which asked for his full name. Anyone might know his date of birth, but only someone who'd researched him thoroughly would know Redmond. "What the hell is this?" he asked, anxiety making his voice even louder than it needed to be to overcome the resistance of the glass partition. "Who are you? What do you want with *me?*"

"This is nothing personal," the blond phantom said, with all the polite charm of Boris Karloff playing a mad murderer in some ancient monochrome melodrama. "I want you to know that. If possible, I'd like you to understand why this is happening, because I think you're entitled to that—but you'll have to be patient, and not interrupt too much. You'll need an open mind, Joe, if you're even to begin to understand."

"I only came to score a handful of Es," Joe said, frantic to make the point. "Strictly for personal consumption. I'm just a user—I'm not in deep. Anyone who says I am is a liar."

"We know exactly what you are," the blond man said, equably. "Don't waste time trying to tell me about yourself—strange as it may seem, I know far more about that than you do. My name is Roland Vane, by the way. I'm an Imperial man myself, as it happens—BSc Psychology 1995."

He can't be only five or six years older than I am! Joe thought. *He doesn't look a day under fifty!* But his panic paused in its rise as he realised that this couldn't really be any kind of drug-war scenario. *What it is,* he told himself, sternly, *is a puzzle. Play it as a game—a PC role-playing game. Don't let all that training go to waste. Life itself is just a blind ride in Virtual Reality. Keep cool.* He was cool enough. It was Thursday night, after all—the nadir of the week—and he was stripped fit for the lab and the Trocadero. An Arcade Ace who could rack up a way-above-average score on his first trip harpooning spacewhales could cope with Roland Vane, BSc and zombie-master.

Aloud, he said: "I didn't know Psychology was such a good line in these materialistic times. Does everyone from the class of '95 own a chauffeur-driven Rolls Royce with all the trimmings?" It seemed like a good line, until he glanced at the man beside him, and felt a renewed chill in the pit of his stomach. The Hulk really didn't look vacant in any *ordinary* way—he actually looked like a twenty-two carat zombie: a brutal body without the least sign of mental activity. The King's Cross buzz was all gone now, and Joe knew that true terror was taking slow possession of him, from top to toe.

"No," the blond man said, lightly. "The others are mostly marking time, waiting for the economy to stop diving into the unplumbed depths of depression. Not that things are any better in organic chemistry, even for people with doctorates. A pity, that—if only ICI or Glaxo-Wellcome were hiring the way they were in the nineties, you might have a bright future in front of you, instead of a life of . . . *crime,* I'm afraid, doesn't quite do justice to the horror of it."

"What the fuck do *you* know about my future?" Joe retorted, knowing even as he framed the question how bizarre it was.

The answer was even more bizarre. "Far too much," said Vane, a little too faintly; Joe had to concentrate hard in order to hear him through the glass. "Everything, and then some. That's how I got to be so rich so quick. To me, the future is an open book, written in blood—but hopefully not in stone. It's an interactive book, you see . . . like one of those choose-your-own-adventure books that were everywhere when I was a kid. You know the PC versions, of course—intimately, according to my information. That's what we're doing, Joe: choosing our own adventure, trying to get through the infinite maze of possibility to the best possible middle."

"You're crazy," Joe said, reflexively. But he knew, as he jerked out the words, that there was some kind of zombie sitting next to him, and that he was in a very, *very* expensive car, and that they knew his middle name—and he was scientist enough to know that a madness with this much method in it was a very methodical madness indeed. Before the blond man could say another word, he blurted out: "What are you going to do with me?"

He didn't get an answer, but he had watched enough *films noirs* to know what it signified when some poor sucker was taken for a ride. He knew what child-proof doors and android wrestlers meant in the melodramatic lexicon of movies and PC games. He couldn't yet quite *believe* it, but he knew.

Perhaps this isn't happening, he thought, dutifully testing out the only other approach. *Perhaps it's not real. Maybe it's some kind of bad trip and I only seem to be awake.*

It wouldn't wash. It was a non-starter, and even if it wasn't . . . the one thing he was certain of was that he had to play the game as if he were playing for his very life.

* * *

Joe studied his surroundings carefully: the rain-spattered windows, the dead screens, polished wood of the minibar, the digital uniphone, the superfax, the CD-ROM apparatus. They were all too distinct to be figments of a dream, but not as precisely-defined and primary-coloured as anything you'd find inside a VR machine. Anyway, the runaway train of his own thoughts was too sharp, too rigorous. No matter how strange and out of control his predicament might be, he was in full possession of *himself.* He could feel the bundle of pills in his pants pocket, and wished that he'd bought something stronger—something strong enough to make all this go away.

"Nobody can see the future," he told the blond man. "All the people who ever claimed they could were just charlatans. It doesn't even make *sense* to believe you can see the future. You get paradoxes."

"I didn't believe it either, Joe," said Roland Vane, still looking ghostly through the glass partition, with Joe's own reflection strangely superimposed on his face. "I'm a scientist, just like you—I need proof before I believe anything, and I need *extra* proof before I believe anything unlikely. But when they kept on feeding me the winners—horses, dogs, shares, headline news, *anything*—there came a time when I had to believe them. When my bank balance was into seven figures, when I had the big house and the classic car, there was no way I could stay sceptical. And that wasn't all. I've seen you sneaking those little sidelong looks at Frank, Joe. You know that there's something *very* creepy about him, don't you? You can tell that someone else is pulling his strings. It's someone way downtime, Joe—someone who's trying to change their past. The downtimers think it can be done, paradoxes or no paradoxes. Even if I didn't believe them, I'd have to go along with them. They've given me a lot of good information, and this is part of the payoff. As I say, it's nothing personal. I really would like you to understand."

With the light on in the back it was impossible to see anything beyond the roller's windows except for the raindrops tracking slantwise across them. Joe hadn't the slightest idea which way they were headed. "Where are we going?" he asked.

"Nowhere," the blond man said—and Joe wished that he didn't believe him.

"You can't do this," Joe said. "You just can't. I don't care what kind of proof you think you have that you're getting messages from the future, and I don't care what kind of a personality problem your over-sized friend has, *you don't have any reason to do this to me!*"

"You have to be stopped, Joe," said the blond man, softly. "You have to be stopped before you get started, or too much damage will be done. It's not just that they want to stop you killing people, Joe—in their time, everybody from nowadays is long-dead anyhow. They're not in the business of merely saving lives, and they're not stupid enough to think that wiping you out will be sufficient to eliminate the joker from the pack. They know that they might have to do this again and again and again, and that every time they do it they run the risk of ripping their own personal threads right out of the loom of fate, *but they have to try.* That's how much damage you're scheduled to do, Joe. You're a *very* dangerous man."

"Try what?" said Joe, faintly, knowing that it wouldn't do any good to keep telling the blond man he was crazy, and that he had to find out more before he could work out a better plan.

"They've been trying to get information back for a long time," Vane said, in his irritating half-whisper. "Years of their time, millennia of ours.

The transmission is problematic, but the reception is the real problem. The receiver has to be a very particular kind of person, you see . . . .it goes without saying that the host mind has to be capable of grasping the concepts involved, so that anyone pre-twentieth century isn't really a candidate, but there are lots of other problems too. Did you ever hear of a French psychologist called Jouvet, Joe?"

"No," said Joe, wondering what chance, if any, he might have to run when the door was finally opened, and whether there was anything to hand that might be used as a weapon, if only he could grab it and wrench it free.

"I thought not," Vane continued, infuriatingly. "Jouvet figured out that a body at the base of the brain called the pons was short-circuiting the messages sent out to the motor system by the brain during dream-sleep. When he removed it, surgically, from the brains of a few experimental cats, he was able to watch the cats acting out their dreams. Sleepwalking in humans is caused by some natural disruption of the functioning of the pons. Ordinarily, you see, people don't act out their dreams—and they don't remember their dreams either, except for a little short-term retention and some dysfunctional imprints. Something somewhere in the brain censors dream-material out from the memory system just as the pons censors the motor signals—and that same something censors out the kind of messages the people of the not-so-distant future will learn to transmit.

"The only people who are good receivers of the kinds of messages the men of the future are sending ,are people whose ability to filter real experience from hallucinatory experience is impaired. Unfortunately, people like that are usually very disturbed people—schizophrenic, dysfunctional people. Anyone born like that is a non-starter in the human race, and the relatively few people who become like it *after* they've learned to function normally tend to write themselves off very quickly. The window of opportunity is very narrow, Joe, and the results of getting the message through are a trifle inconsistent. Frank has his uses for the time being, but they're limited, and the time will very soon arrive when he'll have to be dropped from the team. Peter is a lot more stable, as you can tell from his very capable driving, but when it comes to *understanding*, to the *brainwork*, there's only me. I'm probably the only person in the entire world who can really *dream true*, remember what I dreamed, and integrate it unproblematically with my real experience. I think it might be because I have hardly any dream-life of my own, so there was nothing to confuse, distort or drown out the messages when they started to come through. I never had any imagination, you see—no imagination at all."

Big joke, Joe thought. *If this is having no imagination . . .*

"If dreaming is as essential as some people think," Vane went on, "the signals from the future might actually have saved my sanity, by filling a gap which would otherwise have been damaging. So you see, Joe, I have a lot more to thank the people of the future for than a long list of winning bets . . . although it is an impressively long list. I never win much at any one time, you see, for fear of disrupting the pattern of history too much. The guys downtime want me to be very careful about *unplanned* disruptions, in case some unforeseen change interferes with the ones they desperately want to achieve."

He's telling the truth, Joe thought, wondering at his own capacity for believing the impossible. *Crazy or not, he means every word, and he's going to act on his beliefs with utter conviction. If I'm to get out of this alive, I have to play the game as he defines it. Nothing else will do.* He tried hard to think of a question which would count as a *move,* which might actually give the other man pause—and he felt tremendously proud of his ability to do it. Any straight person, he knew, would be way out of his depth, but a connoisseur's interest in VR games and psychotropic drugs gave a man a different perspective on the life of the senses, with a far higher degree of adaptability built in.

"Do the guys downtime have receivers of their own?" Joe asked.

"Yes they do," said the blond man, whose sudden smile of delight seemed perfectly sincere. "They certainly do."

"And do they get messages from a single future, or from lots of alternatives?" *Jesus, I'm good!* Joe thought. *Is that a hot question or what?*

"The problem," said the blond man, calmly, "is that they don't get any *messages* at all. They get . . . well, think of it as static. The people who are beaming stuff to Frank, Peter and myself are of the opinion that if they can't change the past, there won't *be* any future for humankind—and that's why they're willing to risk eliminating themselves from the pattern of history. They really are serious about this, Joe, and they've done their history homework as carefully as they possibly can."

Joe had played lots of PC games where he was cast as a time-traveller, as a superhero, or even as a demigod. He prided himself on being able to handle any set of rules, and to shift his axiomatic ground as quickly as he could go through the levels. "What you're telling me," he said, serenely, "is that the entire future of mankind somehow rests on me. You think I'm going to do something—*invent* something, I guess—which will wipe out the entire fucking *species*."

"Maybe not quite that drastic," said the blond man, serenely, "but close. There's an awful lot of future from which messages might come, were there anyone capable of sending them. The harm you're presently scheduled to do might not lead to the extinction of the race, but it appears that . . . "

Joe didn't want to hang about. For all he knew they might be only a couple of minutes from their destination. "*Appears* is the operative word," he put in, scornfully. "Has it occurred to the voices in your sleepy little head that they might not be receiving because the guys further downtime have more sense than to send anything, for fear of wiping *themselves* out? Maybe the future is absolutely hunky-dory, and they don't want to rock their cosy little boat. Has it occurred to you or your possibly-imaginary pals that whatever I'm scheduled to invent may be the foundation-stone of a blissfully uncommunicative Utopia?"

For the first time, Vane frowned. *A hit!* Joe thought. *Score one to me!*

"I think I preferred it," the blond man said, almost inaudibly, "when you thought I was mad. I wanted to explain it to you . . . but I suppose, on reflection, it might be better if you *weren't* capable of understanding, or of believing."

Oh shit! Joe thought. *He thinks I'm just as mad as he is—except that because he thinks he's sane, he thinks I'm just as sane as he is . . . which means he thinks that I too might have some kind of hotline to the future . . . but maybe not the same future that his hotline links up to.*

"What exactly," Joe said, "am I scheduled to invent? Are we talking about biological warfare here, or some superpsychotropic that's going to blow everybody's minds, or what?"

"I'm not sure I ought to go into detail about that," the blond man said, uncertainly. The smile was quite gone now.

"I'll bet you aren't," Joe said, softly enough for the other to have to strain to hear him. "You're beginning to sense an Oedipus situation, aren't you? You're beginning to wonder whether your action in trying to *prevent* the prophecy coming true might instead set in train the chain of cause-and-effect that makes it happen."

He grinned, wolfishly, thinking that he had turned disadvantage back into advantage again—but he had overplayed his hand.

"The thought had crossed my mind," Vane admitted, easily enough. "Fortunately, we have the means to prevent the possibility. Oedipus' father was careless enough to leave room for the unfortunate prophecy to be fulfilled—he left the baby on the bare hillside, when a knife through the heart would have settled the matter for good and all. I'm sorry, Joe, but we can't leave anything to chance. The people downtime explained that to me. Above all else, they said, don't try to be subtle; don't mess about with warnings and suggestions—*make sure*. I'm sorry, Joe, but I have to make sure. You do see that, don't you? If you have your own hook-up to a contingent future, you must see it all the more clearly."

It was the first explicit statement Vane had made to confirm that Joe's worst fears were true. He was being taken for a ride in the classic manner, and the intention was that he wouldn't be coming back.

* * *

Joe was able to guess, now, where the roller was headed. Construction workers were adding a sixth westward lane to the M4, widening all the overpasses at the junction with the M25, out near Heathrow. All contract-killed corpses traditionally ended up under motorway bridges. Mr Vane was right—he had no imagination. Even the Silver Shadow now began to look like a clich, to Joe's clear-sighted eyes.

"It won't do any good," Joe said, trying to sound perfectly calm and perfectly confident. "It can't. If your voices exist, so must I. If you were able to rub me out, they couldn't have been able to ask you to do it. You're bound to fail. Worse than that—this *has* to be an Oedipus situation. You're actually playing your historically-allotted part in the tragedy. You're *causing* whatever you're trying to prevent, and so are your friends downtime . . . except, of course, that they're not *really* your friends, are they? They're just using you, the way people do when they want something."

Joe paused for breath and raised his voice, just in case the man beyond the glass wall wasn't getting it all. "There's more to life than backing winning horses, you know, even if we leave aside the fact that your winning streak could stop any minute, and surely will the moment you've done whatever it is the downtimers want you to do. Have you considered the possibility that they might be lying to you? Have you considered the possibility that they might be securing their future instead of trying to abort it? Have you considered the possibility that it's you, not me, that's being taken for a ride?"

Joe racked up his score, although he was well enough aware that at least a couple of his questions lacked real logical clout. He felt morally certain that he was through to the next level now, but there was still a long way to go and in this game he had only one life to lose. He had a bit of a buzz back now, just a hint of a lift, but he was under no illusions about his chances.

If only I could design a drug to do this, he thought, I could make a millions. Imagine a drug which could hype you up for virtual reality to the point where you couldn't tell it from actual reality—something to displace you inside your head as well as out! It could be done—it's just a matter of finding the censor in the brain, and knocking it out for a while. It really could be done, and I could be the guy to do it, if I can only get out of this in one piece.

"I'm sorry, Joe," the blond man said. "There's no way you can talk me out of it. You're history." He smiled again then, and this smile turned into a laugh.

The fact that the thin man could laugh at such a pathetically feeble joke made Joe angry. He wasn't playing fair!

"If your voices really are all that's keeping you sane," Joe pointed out, changing tack again with dogged persistence, "you could lose more than a hotline to an ace racing tipster. You could lose your marbles too. You aren't playing this like a clever punter, are you? A *sensible* man would string them along, spin it out. A real horseplayer would say 'Sure I'll do what you want, but not quite yet.' You really ought to think about your own future prospects, your own security."

"I wish I could," said Vane. "Unfortunately, it wouldn't do any good. I already have an appointment with destiny that can't be ducked. You've probably noticed that I look a little older than I am. That's because I'm suffering from a form of progeria—that's a fancy term for premature aging. Some glitch in my DNA-spectrum means that my chromosome-complement doesn't copy accurately enough when my cells divide, and errors accumulate at a greater than normal rate. I only have six months to live, Joe, a year at the most—and it won't be fun. When I decide to opt out, a few weeks or a few months downtime, I'll use the same gun that Peter's going to use on you. There'll be a certain justice in that, don't you think? A certain *neatness*."

"It doesn't leave you much time to hit the next guy," Joe observed, switching strategies yet again, with the practised ease of an authentic

Arcade Ace. "The guy who'll become the inventor of whatever-it-is once I'm out of the picture. There will be another guy, won't there? That's what you meant earlier when you said that your voices might have to do it over and over again. You and your voices should know full well that you can't unmake a scientific discovery whose time has come. If I don't hit the jackpot, someone else will."

"Perhaps," said the blond man, agreeably. "Maybe we're all helpless, and there's nothing anyone can do to make the world better than it is, or better than it might be. But we have to try, don't we? We *do* have to try."

To his horror, Joe realised that the car was slowing down, coming smoothly to a halt. *This is it,* he thought. *No lives left, and no way of knowing what score is showing on the board.*

"Get out," said the blond man, softly.

Joe made no move to obey, but it made no difference. The driver was already out, and walking around the car. Frank had come to life again—as near to life as he ever got. Joe groped at the fittings, trying to yank the phone clear of the console, but he didn't have a chance against the pressure of Frank's huge hands. When Peter opened the child-proof door, the zombie shoved Joe out, empty-handed, to sprawl on the muddy ground.

* * *

I won't go down meekly, Joe thought, as he scrambled in the slippery mud, trying to get back on his feet. *They can kill me, but I'm damned if I'll just stand by and wait for them to do it.* He was possessed by rage, and all his attention was focused on the project of leaping forward to attack Roland Vane: to shove his finger's into the blond man's eyes; to sink a knee into his prematurely-aged balls. For Joe, if not for his adversary, this was very personal indeed.

But the power of desire wasn't enough. As soon as Joe was on his feet the Incredible Hulk grabbed him again, and held him still, seemingly without any effort at all.

With his arms pinned to his sides Joe was brought around to face Vane and the driver. The wind was blowing rain into his face, and he had to blink, but there was light enough from the Silver Shadow's blazing head-lamps to show him the lightly-jaundiced colour of Vane's face. There was no glass wall between them now, but Vane looked as ghostly as ever.

The man called Peter was holding a gun: one of those Red Army revolvers that had been the Russian black market's principal westward export for the last fifteen or twenty years.

"I really am sorry, Joe," Vane said. "I know you're innocent, as yet, but prevention is always better than punishment, and you'll just have to take it from me that this will save you from becoming a truly evil man. If you have a soul, Joe, this little surgical operation might save it from the darkest depths of hell.

Joe struggled with all might against Frank's grip, but he might as well have tried to turn back time.

He saw Peter lift the gun, and he heard a shot which sounded like the crack of doom. His eyes closed, reflexively, and he waited, squeamishly, for the pain to begin. He was horribly afraid of the pain.

He heard a cry of anguish, and for a moment thought that it must be his own—but when he opened his eyes again, Peter had fallen, and it was Vane who was wailing while he scrabbled in the mud for the gun.

Joe struggled to take in the implications.

Vane couldn't pick up the revolver. Maybe Peter had gripped it too tightly as the spasm of death took hold of him, or perhaps the mud made it too slick to grasp. For whatever reason, Vane couldn't get it free in time. Joe blinked away an inconvenient raindrop just in time to see a round red mark appear in the blond man's forehead, an instant before the back of his head exploded.

Frank was too stupid to turn around, although it was obvious enough to Joe that the gunman must be behind them. All the zombie did was relax his grip, allowing Joe to squirm free and dive. Joe didn't even try to look back—he just kept his head well down while three more shots rang out. Somehow, he had known that there would be three: the giant wasn't the kind of man who'd go down in one. Mercifully, when he finally fell he didn't fall on top of Joe.

Strike three! Joe thought, as he heard the squelchy sound of the big man's body hitting the muddy ground. "Game Over and a new record score! What a hit!"

He wasn't surprised, when he wiped his face after getting to his feet, to see that the assassin was a woman. He could have wished that she was better-looking—she looked almost old enough to be his mother—but this was real life, after all, and she was handsome enough in a body-builderish sort of way. Her black hair would probably have looked sleek if it weren't for the pouring rain, and she would probably have been wearing seriously sexy clothes if she hadn't come out dressed to kill, in a jet black waterproof track-suit and Nike trainers. Her gun was an automatic; Joe didn't recognise the make.

Joe's saviour knelt down to start stripping the bodies of their ID. When she'd finished, she threw a set of car-keys to Joe, but they weren't the keys to the Rolls. That was good thinking, he figured, having by now collected his scattered wits. The Silver Shadow would be far too conspicuous to take back into town, and it would be very difficult for him to account for his possession of it if he were stopped.

"It's a red Clio, parked behind the bulldozer," the woman told him. She looked far less spectral than Roland Vane, and sounded as if she had everything under control. It was evident that not everyone who was wired up to the future turned into a freak.

"Can I help you with the bodies?" Joe asked, politely.

"You'll have to give me a hand with Frank's," she said. "The others are no trouble. The hole's just over here. I'll fill it in myself—I like driving the heavy stuff and the concrete's ready-mixed."

It wasn't difficult for the two of them to roll the enormous zombie into the waiting hole—Peter had obligingly driven them almost to the lip. Joe helped her with the others anyhow, although she could have moved them herself.

"I know this is a terrible line," said Joe, as Vane tumbled into the waiting pit, "but have we met before?"

"Only in your dreams," she answered.

"I can never remember my dreams," he told her. "I guess I'm not really cut out for this kind of game."

"There's a knack to it," she told him. "Getting started is the hard part, but it can be learned, if you have the motivation—and a good teacher."

She was standing still now, waiting for him to go. She was really quite handsome, in spite of her age and all the mud that was clinging to her. Joe briefly reminded himself of all the rumoured advantages of making love to older women.

"How do I get the car back to you?" he asked.

"I'll collect it," she assured him. "Not tomorrow, or the next day, but soon. Don't worry about a thing. Have a good time at the party tomorrow night."

"Who are you?" he asked, expecting exactly the kind of answer he got.

"I'm your guardian angel," she said, in a voice heavy with sexy sarcasm. "You're going to be hard work, I know, but it'll be worth it. We have a tough job to do, but we'll make a great team. You have a wonderful future in front of you, if you play your cards right. Now go."

"Am I really going to cause the deaths of millions of people?" he asked, hesitantly wondering if he ought to care more than he did. What were these hypothetical downtimers, after all, but phantoms in some VR game?

"Joe," she said, with a real cutting edge to her voice, "you and I are going to cause the death of millions of *universes*. That's what making choices means. You'll be a fully human being soon. There aren't many of us about yet, but take it from me . . . this is just the beginning. Now *go*, before you catch a chill and abort a billion fabulous futures. I promise I'll see you soon."

Obediently, he turned away.

He began to walk, with the rain lashing at his back, knowing that it always ended this way, whether it was a game or a movie or a ride. The hero always came through, always lived to fight another day. In any case, what he had told the blond man must be true. What had already happened, from the future's point of view, *had to happen*. Nothing else made sense. Surely Vane and the guardian angel were just filling in the fine detail of a history already on record.

It was dark in the shadow of the bulldozer; the Clio was just a black blur, and he had to grope for the door handle and fiddle the key into the lock. He couldn't help looking around nervously, wondering if there might yet be a third gang of assassins, waiting to overtrump the woman's winning play. A whole legion could have been hiding in the gloom, beyond the curtain of driving rain, but he told himself again that nothing disastrous could happen. He told himself sternly that the partition between the present and the future couldn't possibly be shattered, even if the people of the future would one day contrive to see through it, because men of different ages were just phantoms to one another . . . but he couldn't shake off the tingling unease, even when the Clio's door opened and the interior light came on.

Ah, what the hell! he thought, as he got into the car. *So what if it's true? If all reality is virtual from this day forward, and all the actors of the stage of history just icons to be shot at, who better to survive and thrive than an Arcade Ace who knows the value of Ecstasy?*

He laughed then. The idea that all future history might become a game for expert dreamers to play was by no means unappealing, seen in the right light.

He was, after all, a child of his time.

I always knew I was destined for something like this, he thought, as he fastened his seat-belt. *I always knew that there was something more, something better, something that really mattered. I always knew that I was destined to be on the inside, that all the practice I put in on all the games couldn't be for nothing, and couldn't be allowed to go to waste.*

He turned the key in the ignition. He neither heard nor felt the explosion that abruptly ripped the car apart and blew his body and brain to fleshy shreds.

It was, in its fashion, the most merciful of all possible fates.

VIRTUOUS REALITY

I kept no reckoning of time or place, and the stars of my fate faded from heaven, and therefore the earth grew dark and its figures passed before me like flitting shadows, and among them all I beheld only—Morella. [Edgar Allan Poe, "Morella"]

I will admit, if you like, that I am old-fashioned, or even that I was born out of my time. But you must understand that to someone like me, who learned to love bound books more than textplates, holovideo shows and Virtual Reality synthetapes, the ideas and values of ancient times are every bit as real and present to my mind as the ideas and values of the twenty-third century, and not one whit less worthy. That is the greatest gift of intelligence, technology and civilization: that humans are not bound to one moment or to one place, but have the power to understand and embrace the alienness of elsewhere and elsewhen.

I am not a product of perverted education, to be reckoned an obsessive freak; my co-parents certainly encouraged my antiquarian interests but they did not force their collection of antique books upon me, nor did they inhibit my use of modern communications technology. I consider myself to be a self-made man, and I do not think that there is anything regrettable in the fact that many of my attitudes and emotions are made in the image of a characteristic mindset of the distant past.

It is difficult for modern people to get to grips, intellectually and imaginatively, with the notion that the mental life of our ancestors was very unlike our own, but it is true. The fact that we continue to employ the same words in different contexts helps to obscure and conceal these differences, but there is not the slightest doubt that what the people of the nineteenth and twentieth centuries meant by "love" or "passion" was something much richer, more profound and more vivid than what those words now signify to most of us. I have always taken pride in my ability not merely to comprehend but also to *feel* the meanings which such words as those once had, but have no more. The people of those distant times were far less cerebral than the common herd of today, and their emotions had a power to excite and consume which would seem utterly alien to all but a few inhabitants of our more solemn and orderly era.

When I say that I came to love Morella, therefore, I do not mean to refer to the kind of calm affection which my neighbours presumably feel for the various members of their organic households.

These days, the statistics assure us, the average American male has three point six wives at any one time, and—assuming the average rate of turnover in the various households with which he associates himself—can expect to have ninety-three point five wives altogether, in the course of a lifetime which includes the usual two rejuvenations. As rejuvenation technology improves and child licences become more difficult to obtain these figures are likely to increase steadily, and this will undoubtedly make monogamy even more unfashionable in times to come. But my love for Morella was of an older and finer kind which could not tolerate the thought of any alliance save for monogamy.

My soul burned for Morella, with a fire which was painful and yet exalting; and I knew from the very first that fate had bound us together, exclusively and inextricably.

Morella was perfectly content, in the beginning, with the kind of arrangement which I proposed to her. She was only seventeen years old—I was thirty—but she was possessed of great intelligence and an astonishing intensity of concentration. She had already become estranged from her co-parents, who considered her unco-operative and antisocial. (I believe that this will increasingly come to be seen as a normal pattern as child licences become more difficult to obtain; the solitary children of groups of eight or ten parents will inevitably come to see themselves as aliens within their own homes, and will increasingly retreat—as Morella did—into the synthetic worlds of Virtual Reality whose counterfeit experience becomes more convincing and more varied with every year that passes.)

Morella and I were, I think, far more similar in our interests and inclinations than we seemed to outside observers. She had no particular love for books before I met her—her ability to handle encoded text was in no way impaired, but she employed it in a strictly functional capacity—but the Virtual Realities which she most loved to visit were those which set out to re-create the pre-cinematic world in all the fullness of its primitive and magical glory. We educated one another in the sharing of our passions; I taught her the processes of conjuration by which the ancient threads of words could be spun into a wondrous garment of mental experience; she showed me that even the relatively crude Virtual Reality simulations which were then in common use were also worthy collaborators with the human imagination.

Although we preferred to look through different windows, Morella and I loved to look out upon the same lost world, and we were happy to talk endlessly about our experiences, enriching one another's understanding with our complementary accounts. I am convinced that her love for me was, in the beginning and in its fullest bloom, as beautifully and as powerfully anachronistic as mine for her.

We shared our experiences as fully as we could. Although she never became a habitual reader, she was delighted to listen while I read aloud to her the poetry of bygone ages. I, in my turn, would partner her in those adventures in Virtual Reality which were designed to be collaborative. These were, of course, new and few in those days, but we readily invested in more sophisticated equipment as and when it became available. I had always shunned synthetic visual and tactile experiences before, thinking them too crude to interest one as sensitive as myself, but it soon came to seem, even to me, that when Morella and I donned our co-ordinated data suits we were as closely united as we were when we caressed one another in the flesh.

To Morella, I have no doubt, setting forth together into some Alternative World was the most perfect form of our intimacy, and the real core of our union. Together, we roamed the picturesque (and, it must be admitted, somewhat impressionistic) streets of Dickens' London, Baudelaire's Paris and D'Annunzio's Rome; and when the artistry of the synthesisers increased we were among the first armchair pioneers to explore the wildernesses of Livingstone's Africa, Scott's Antarctica and Lowell's Mars. The simulations were far from perfect, but we refused to recognise their imperfections.

There was no limit to our ambition; the simulation of contemporary environments was technically much better, but it was always the most exotic milieux which attracted us. When cosmic voyage tapes first became available we immediately discounted those based in contemporary astronomical theory, and became aficionados of that esoteric species which dealt with outdated models of the universe. Together, we abandoned our bodies to take flight into the cosmos of Poe's *Eureka* and Camille Flammarion's *Lumen*. There, our carefully-educated collaborative imagination found a unique opportunity to sense that which is truly fundamental to mankind's awareness of the enormity of the universe. Of all the synthetapes we owned, it was those wild flights of obsolete but grandiose fancy which we found most inspiring—and, oddly enough, most convincing. Although they were eccentric fictions, replete with ideas discredited by subsequent advances in science, they seemed to both of us to contain a particular awesomeness, a very special sense of the infinite and the eternal, which passage of time and the march of earthly progress had not devalued in the least.

We were happy, Morella and I.

I thought—and I sincerely believed, with all my heart—that we could be happy forever. I could have been. I had that kind of strength. But Morella, for all her fascination with antiquity, was much more a child of her era than I ever was. Her love for me began gradually to cool, and to transform itself into the kind of tolerant benevolence which our contemporaries consider to be normal and desirable.

She *did* still love me; of that there is no doubt. But she wanted to love other people too; she wanted to take a more active part in society; she wanted to look to the future as well as the past. All this she said, and more. She had become as dissatisfied with our reclusive life of study and leisure as she had formerly become with the eventful riot of life in the household where she had been raised. She felt that it was time to look for work of some kind, time to undertake new experiments in lifestyle, time to see new places as they actually were, without the aid of a Virtual Reality hood.

I understood what she said, but I was hurt. I cannot entirely explain the subsequent alteration of my feelings towards her. I certainly never stopped loving her, and my love never underwent the kind of transmutation—the horrific decay, as it seemed to me—to which hers was subject, but the temper of my own passion changed nevertheless. I loved her utterly, devotedly, fiercely; and yet, as her total devotion to me began to falter, it soon came about that I could no longer bear the touch of her slender fingers, nor the low tone of her musical voice, nor the lustre of her melancholy eyes.

She *was* melancholy, on my behalf, because she saw all too clearly what the dilution of her love was doing to me.

We continued to live our life, for a while. We were still avid to acquire and use every new synthetape of the particular kind we loved best. In the dark and marvellous cosmos of the nineteenth century imagination, where we existed as disembodied souls of the kind Flammarion had described, we were incarnated on a dozen different worlds, in alien forms exoskeletal and endoskeletal, sentient and semiconscious, organic and inorganic. I could not help thinking of this, sometimes, as a search for that one paradisal Virtual Reality—which I secretly labelled the Virtuous Reality—in which we would recover the fundamental harmony of our souls, and thus be saved from the dissolution of our marriage.

Alas, there was no such destiny for us.

When we were not adventuring in obsolete universes, I continued to read to her all the most gorgeous and sentimental words penned by the Romantic poets: all the most exquisitely-wrought verbal symphonies of the past. By this means too I sought a magic spell which might reignite the fire of our mutual passion, but it was all too obvious that Morella's growing indifference was reducing the words to mere plaintive and desolate echoes.

It was inevitable that she would leave, and I had to accept it. She would go out into the world to join an organic household, where she would have four or five co-husbands and as many co-wives, while I would be alone . . . forever.

It was on an autumnal evening, when the winds lay still in heaven, that she departed.

"I will never forget," she promised me. "What we have shared will always be a treasure to me. What you have taught me will always be part of me, and I am glad that I have walked *with you* in the wilder pastures of Infinity."

I kissed her forehead, but could not speak.

"I must go," she said, "but you will have me still, in your memory. We have had as many years as the lovers of old, who were all-too-soon parted by disease and death. They came to this pass as naturally as we have come, and such moments as this were part and parcel of the pain of their finite hearts."

"Morella!" I whispered, but could say no more.

"Goodbye, my love," she murmured, as she turned her back.

It was not until she had been gone for several days—or perhaps for several months—that I began to realise how true her words were. At first, I was plunged into a pit of despair. Whatever I did, wherever I went, I felt her absence. Whenever I took up a book to read, the one thought present in my mind was that I was reading silently *because Morella was not there.* I never entered the room where we had assembled our Virtual Reality apparatus, because I knew that I would see two data suits, and that there would be no one with me. I could not bear to think of venturing *alone* into ancient streets, let alone the darkness of ancient infinity.

It seemed, for a dreadful interval, that when Morella had gone my life had gone with her, and that I had been left with nothing but the dust and ashes of my existence.

But I was wrong, and she was right. In the long-gone days when all men—or the best of them, at least—felt as I had schooled myself to feel, the grief of parting was a common thing, which had to be faced with courage. To live as I had undertaken to live, in a stormy private world of wild desire and brittle hope, required a definite inner fortitude, and a proper appreciation of the preciousness of all things briefly held and lost again. I saw, eventually, that although Morella was gone, the glory of our love could never be annihilated while memory preserved it.

She had spoken the simple truth when she sought to reassure me, and to soften the blow of her departure. Memory was the key to the problem which faced me. What, after all, were the texts which I loved so dearly but memory made incarnate, memory crystallised, memory enshrined? What were the synthetapes whose evolution we had followed so keenly but brave attempts to supplement and enrich those incarnate memories, to re-place the dimensions of touch and vision which text could never carry?

I began to repair my loss in the simplest possible way: I began to read aloud again, just as if Morella were there. While my eyes were fixed upon the ancient pages all else was invisible; the matter of her actual presence simply did not arise. I read *to her.* You may think of it as pretence, if you will, but it was not that; it was an authentic conquest of circumstance by imagination. I told myself that, and meant it.

There was a moment of hesitation, I suppose, before I was able to take this revelation to its logical conclusion. There must have been a pause when I said to myself: "What a pity it is that the same stratagem would not work with a synthetape, where the eyes are not held captive by text, and where the absence of my beloved would be manifest." But it was only a moment: a fleeting instant of thoughtlessness. I must have seen immediately what a fool I was to think that; when the realisation came to me it must have come as a blinding flash of enlightenment, which made me feel utterly ridiculous for not having seen it before.

What I saw was this: that the words and images biochemically graven in my brain were not the only set of memories that Morella had left behind. She had left behind a very different, and complementary set, in the adaptive programmes which had adjusted her data suit to her form and her movements.

I knew, of course, that there already existed countless synthetapes which reproduced the sensations of social, and sexual, intercourse—that Virtual Realities could include synthetic persons as well as synthetic landscapes and universes. Such sensations were as crude and incomplete as all other Virtual Realities were, but they only required the same input of imagination, the same willing suspension of disbelief, to function. Had I wanted to, I could have commissioned the modification of a standard sextape so that the female image therein was moulded to the image of Morella, but that was exactly what I did *not* want to do. That would have been a kind of self-betrayal, a deliberate acceptance of the ersatz. What I wanted—what I needed—was something infinitely more subtle.

I did the work myself, instructed in method and planning by the datanet, assisted by microrobotic circuit workers trained by standard skillpacks. My mechanical servants and I patiently and ingeniously re-wired the data suit which Morella had used—which no one *but* Morella had ever used—so that even though it remained empty it would project into any synthetape the perfect image of a hypothetical collaborator, built out of all the recordings it had made in the course of projecting the image of the actual Morella into our many adventures in the reconstituted past.

It is true that the Morella who was thus enabled to accompany me into all the worlds which we had previously entered, and all the new worlds which came on to the market week by week, was not quite *whole*. She was unable to innovate in conversation, and the repertoire of her movements and physical responses was both limited and stereotyped, but *she was the real Morella*. She was not some simulacrum painted by a synthetape artist working from photographs and other dead data. She was a reincarnate memory whose new existence was contiguous with her former one and which had evolved out of it in a natural manner. She did not quite have Morella's mind, but she had Morella's soul.

In existential terms, I was prepared to meet her half way. I only had to do as she did, and be as she was, to secure a union of equals, eternal and indivisible.

Thus it was that while still living, I embarked upon a kind of afterlife. I set out to live in the myriad alternative worlds contained in books and tapes—and as the acids in the paper gradually consumed my collection of ancient artifacts in spite of all my efforts to preserve them, I turned more and more frequently to the tapes. I cut myself adrift from the present, and turned my back upon the future. I kept little reckoning of time or place, and the earth itself seemed to grew dark, becoming phantasmal, so that its figures passed before me like flitting shadows. Among them all I beheld only—Morella.

With Morella, I explored the mysteries of the ages; with Morella, I explored the wonders of the firmament; with Morella, I lived a thousand lives on a thousand worlds; with Morella I tasted the sweet fruits of Heaven and the fiery liquors of Hell.

With Morella, I found my Virtuous Reality. It is here, and it is now; it is everywhere, and everything, and *evermore.*

WILDLAND

Burslem and Okuyama came to the surface of the Earth from the city of Chicago Underground in the year which, according to the calendar they kept, was 3856 years after the advent of the ice. The ice, of course, was long gone—retired to the poles by the activity of the Wildland—but it had been the return of the ice following the failure of the legendary Greenhouse Plan which had forced the Tripartite Division of mankind, which had in turn given birth to the Cities Underground. It was, therefore, entirely natural that the citizens of those deep-set caverns should count the years of their history from that vital moment.

The purpose of the two men was to gather certain specimens which were required by the Exobiological Research Institute, in which they served as Scientific Officers. The Institute had been founded more than two thousand years earlier, commissioned to investigate the possibility of reclaiming the surface of the Earth from the alien Wildland. It had made steady progress in understanding the biology of the invading ecosystem, but there was as yet no viable plan by which humans might seek to regain ecological hegemony over the world which they still considered to be theirs.

Burslem and Okuyama's mission was a routine one, which neither man had any reason to regard as being of particular importance; but every journey into the Wildland was fraught with danger, and no such mission could be treated casually.

The two men wore sterile suits which isolated them entirely from the Wildland, sheathing their bodies in tough plastic. The water-bags and food-drip packs inside each suit would last for fourteen days; the waste-recycling apparatus would in theory sustain a man for a further ten days if necessary, but the biochemical side-effects of such emergency sustenance were uncomfortable and to a degree unpredictable. Time, therefore, was of the essence—as it was whenever a mission took men far from the airlocks which linked the underworld to the World Above.

Despite their common cause, the two men differed considerably. They contrasted even in appearance, for Burslem was much the burlier of the two, but the more important contrast was in their attitudes to the Wildland.

Burslem had always been fascinated by the alien life-system, and had joined the Institute in order to discover everything he could about it. He thought the Wildland fabulously beautiful, and loved wandering there; he found an aesthetic delight in the wonders of its biochemical genetics, which were so much more subtle, flexible and powerful than the genetic systems of Earth's native life. To the supposed aim of the Institute—the utter destruction of the Wildland—he paid respectful lip service, but he knew that this was not an aim likely to be fulfilled in his own time, or even in the remote future. He knew that in any war between the Wildland and men, the Wildland would be the victor, and he had sworn loyalty to the Institute's cause mainly in order to gain the opportunity to learn more about the object of his fascination.

Okuyama, on the other hand, considered the Wildland to be the ultimate evil. He hated and loathed it, and the object of *his* enquiries into its nature was the faint hope that one day he or another might make that crucial breakthrough which would allow its destruction.

Both these attitudes were unrepresentative. The vast majority of the inhabitants of the Cities Underground had no interest at all in the surface of the Earth, and could not have cared less whether that surface was in the grip of an Ice Age or an alien invader, or whether it was only a charming myth that the Earth *had* a surface. (This view was actually held by a few eccentric cultists, who asserted that the universe was an infinite solid with occasional lacunae, and believed that the myth of the surface was maintained by the scientific elite simply as a means of winning prestige.) Most underworlders were entirely content with the underworld, and could imagine no other way of life. If their uncivilized ancestors had once lived on the surface, that merely went to prove how uncivilized they were.

The possibility (seriously feared by such as Okuyama) that the

Wildland would one day invade the underworld and consume it just as it had consumed the surface biosphere, was not taken seriously by ordinary people, who had complete faith in the airlocks, and had not the intellectual capacity to imagine such a disaster. Underground life had severely constricted the imaginative horizons of most men—on this point Burslem and Okuyama would have agreed. It was the only matter on which they did agree; they did not like one another, and perhaps it was a mistake to send them out together.

* * *

At first, Burslem and Okuyama's work went smoothly. The region close to the airlocks was not so densely forested as many, perhaps because the streets and buildings of Old Chicago had once stood here, and their disintegration had left a vile soil which even the Wildland could not make fecund. The very sparseness of the local *flora*, however, made it necessary for the two explorers to venture further afield, into the valley which had once been Lake Michigan before the Wildland had absorbed the greater part of its waters.

They passed, therefore, from relatively open terrain into the crowded forest, laying traps as they went. The traps would hopefully contain motiles when they picked them up on the return journey. Occasionally they paused to gather florets and filaments, or chisel away strips of bark, though their real goal was to gather more exotic specimens.

As they proceeded, it became gradually more difficult to force a way through the Wildland's undergrowth, and the machetes with which they hacked at the impeding vegetation were blunted by the ligneous stems. Their suits became smeared with sticky sap, and it was often necessary to stop and clean their eyepieces. There were traps set by the Wildland, too, which they had to avoid—cunningly concealed pitfalls and whiplashing vines.

By the end of their second day, they were very tired. It was hard labour indeed to build the fire which they must keep alive all night, because it would keep at bay with flame and smoke some of the insectile elements of the Wildland which, if given time, might chew right through the plastic of their suits and let the Wildland in.

"This work should be done by robots," said Okuyama, morosely. "It should not be necessary to risk men. We have lost nine in the last seven years—even Rogulski, who knew this awful wilderness better than any of us."

Privately, Burslem thought that it would be a terrible shame to be banned from this wonderful place, but that was not a view he dared present to Okuyama. Instead, he said: "The robots cannot do the job. The Wildland quickly finds ways to frustrate them, and they are very expensive to produce. It may be a harsh judgment, but given the scope of our resources, men are more expendable than such sophisticated machines."

"That is a terrible attitude," Okuyama told him. "We should count human life more precious than that."

"I do not say that I think it myself," Burslem replied. "I merely observe that such calculations are understandable."

"New York and Miami have the benefit of the sub-Atlantic tunnels, and their miners supply them more than adequately with vital inorganics. If they were not so tight-fisted in their trading with Chicago, we would have resources enough. If the Wildland is to be defeated all men must work together, instead of striving for advantage, man over man and city over city."

"Rivalry between neighbours and between cities is of far greater importance to most underworlders than the eventual conquest of the Wildland," said Burslem, tiredly. "They price comfort far above knowledge, and grudge us their support. It is the way things are, and it is useless to complain. We do what we can."

They pressurized their bubble-tent and rigged their alarms, then settled down to sleep. They slept lightly, in spite of their tiredness, surrounded as they were by dangers. Shortly after dawn their drips released an alarm call of stimulant psychochemicals, and they bundled up their kit with quick efficiency.

As they moved out into the Michigan basin they had to quit the ground and make their way up into the forest canopy.

Because the "trees" of the Wildland were not separate entities their branches often fused, making highways far above the ground which were used by the larger motiles. The mid-growth of the forest was denser than the undergrowth, at least around the giant trunks which were the Wildland's skeleton. There was more colour here, too; very little light penetrated to the ground and the undergrowth was all greys and browns, while the mid-growth showed countless pastel shades of red, blue and gold. The greens of the high canopy formed a complex geometrical pattern against the blue sky, letting the light through in a carefully ordered way.

The mid-growth also concealed more dangers for the travellers to watch out for. Nettlenets and stinging anemones could not hurt them in their suits, nor did they need to fear the Wildland's battery of poisons, but there were gluegaws and bowerconstrictors to be avoided, and there was always the possibility of a fall. The higher they went, the further there was to fall, and though there was plenty of vegetation between themselves and the ground, it was not always possible to halt or slow a fall well enough to avoid broken limbs.

They were threatened once by an arachnoid—an eight-legged thing which straddled an open space between three relatively bare trunks, thirty metres from tip to tip, though its "body" was only a couple of metres in diameter. Okuyama drew his gun and put three bullets into it, but it simply withdrew, in leisurely fashion, into the high canopy, dripping ichor as it went. It was not a true animal, of course—nothing in the Wildland was. When it returned to the tree which had spawned it, which was presumably close by, it would merge its flesh with its parent, and its tissues would be patiently renewed.

Later, they watched from a distance as an arachnoid and a frogling fought on a great palmate leaf high above them. The frogling was bigger and more mobile, and had its long tongue to use as a weapon, but it was an unequal contest and once the arachnoid had begun to tie the frogling down with the silk that flooded from its spinnerets, the issue was settled.

Why such fights went on, the humans were still not sure. Some theorists believed that the Wildland was best regarded as a single gargantuan organism, and that all the individuals which it modelled on the Earthly creatures it had long ago ingested were simply units of its body, like cells or organelles. If this was true, then the destruction of one motile by another could be seen only in terms of internal regulation and waste-disposal. Others believed, though, that there were many individuals in the Wildland, still involved in their own struggle for existence, and that the struggle had almost been resolved—not according to the logic of the survival of the fittest and the extinction of the less fit, but by the ecological equivalent of a treaty, in which the individuals traded genetic materials even while retaining, in some enigmatic sense, their own identities. If this were true, then the devouring of some motiles by others could be seen either as a fading atavistic echo, or as part of the pattern of genetic trading.

Burslem often devoted long hours of his spare time to deliberation upon this problem. Okuyama did not care much one way or the other.

* * *

When they were high enough in the canopy, Burslem and Okuyama selected what seemed to be a fairly young "tree" and began to assemble the telescopic tap which could be driven, with much effort, deep into its body. Their intention was to drive a hollow metal tube through the bark and ligneous tissue of the trunk into the pithy heart where the "nucleus" was, in order to draw off some of the genetic soup within. Nearer to the ground the trunks were far too thick, and even at this level an old trunk was likely to be so tough as to make the job very difficult indeed, but the young, slender trunk which they had found seemed unlikely to present them with too stern a task. They took turns with the hammer-drill, first Burslem and then Okuyama. It was while Burslem was preparing to take his second turn that he noticed the bronzed face watching them from a tangle of blooms twenty metres away on a horizontal bough.

Burslem dropped the drill, and took a step toward the watcher, then cursed himself silently for giving away the fact that he was aware of the other's presence. The face disappeared, and he broke into a run, racing along the branch with a reckless disregard for its thinness. He plunged pell-mell into the clump of red florets, groping for something more solid than the slender curled stems that bore them. He clutched something, but could not tell whether it was an arm or a leg. It twisted, trying to escape his grip, and the movement of the other body pulled him deeper into the florets, but he dug his fingers in as hard as he could, determined not to lose his prey.

He lost his balance, but concentrated entirely on trying to get his other hand on the wriggling form which he had so unexpectedly managed to capture. He caught what felt like an ankle, and now both his hands were clinging tight. He felt such a burst of joy and triumph that he did not realise immediately that both he and his captive had tumbled from the tangle of blooms, and were falling.

He was undermost, and the wind was knocked out of him as his back collided with another branch, but he did not let go. He gasped for air, feeling as if his chest were in a vice, his lungs unable to draw. His shoulders were battered again as he fell into something softer and springier, but it was not enough to break the fall. It did, however, cause the pair of them to tumble in mid-fall, so that now it was the other who was underneath.

When they cannoned again into something hard it was not Burslem who took the brunt of the impact. Agonized by his attempts to suck air into his lungs, though, he felt as if the plastic of the sterile suit were choking him, and the iron will that was forcing his hands to retain their fierce clutch suddenly died in him. He felt his body relaxing, and as he finally managed to get a breath of oxygen his sense of triumph turned to a conviction of defeat. Then the fall was abruptly stopped by a final solid impact, and the other body jerked free. Dizzily, he cursed himself again, more spitefully than he had thought possible.

* * *

By the time that Okuyama reached Burslem he was able to breathe again, and although he could not find the energy to sit up he thought that his limbs were probably unbroken. He had not entirely lost consciousness, but felt light-headed and remote, not fully in contact with his body.

Without ceremony, Okuyama bundled him over, checking his suit for damage before prodding his arms and legs with an inquiring finger.

"You're okay," he said, finally.

"I lost him," complained Burslem. "I had him, and I lost him."

"No you didn't," Okuyama told him. "And as far as appearances are concerned, it's a she. It's flat out with a twisted leg. Broken, I suppose, if it has bones to break."

Burslem sat bolt upright, and looked around. They were on a broad, spatulate bough in the middle canopy, cushioned by fernlike excrescences. About a metre away was the form of the person he had grappled with, looking for all the world like a sixteen-year-old girl with tanned skin and blonde hair. She was quite naked, and looked entirely human—which of course she was not.

"There are supposed to be no dryads in these latitudes," he murmured. "No one out of Chicago ever brought in hard evidence. I never believed the sightings. Imagination, I thought. Is she dead?"

Okuyama shrugged. "Doubt it," he said. "Nothing its tree couldn't put right, if it could get back to it. Up to us to see that doesn't happen—don't want it dissolving before our very eyes. Got to get it back, and carefully too. Wrap it up in the bubble-tent, I guess. Got to keep it out of contact, just in case. Do you suppose it can *talk*?"

"I don't think so. When they pushed through the subatlantic cable New York's datasystems interfaced with Europe's, and the French fed back some stuff about attempts to make contact with the Wildmen in North Africa. All the indications are that the Wildmen are mindless. You think the trees have traded genomes all the way from the tropics? Can *these* trees produce Wildmen now? Must be, I guess. She can't have come all the way from the Amazon, can she?"

"It's not a she," Okuyama corrected him, roughly. "It's not human. It's a bit of an alien plant, right? And it doesn't mean us any good. Hell, Bur—you think there are any more around? You think they'll try to get it back?"

Burslem frowned. Despite his enthusiasm to know everything about the Wildland that could be dug out of the datasystems, and notwithstanding a particular fascination with the notion of humanoid motiles, he knew very little about dryads that might help him to answer Oyukama's question. He rose to his feet, painfully and a little unsteadily. He was battered and bruised, but he could walk.

"We've got to get the equipment," he said. "We'll abandon the tap and start back right away. We've got to get her home. She's worth more than a bucketful of gene-soup. I think you're right about the bubble-tent. You go get it—I'll stand guard here." He took the gun from his holster, and checked that the fall hadn't damaged it.

Okuyama nodded, and began to make his way back up the trunk, scaling it by means of the rope which he had fastened in order to make the descent.

Burslem looked around, carefully, anxious to spot any other watching faces, but there seemed to be nowhere close at hand where they might hide. He knelt beside the immobile form, and touched the dryad's arm, but she did not stir. He put the plastic covering the back of his left hand close to her mouth, attempting to detect the condensation of her breath, but he was not even certain that she *did* breathe. The Wildland often reproduced outward form without inward structure. Internally, an arachnid was nothing like a spider, though a frogling *was* recognisably similar to a frog. Maybe the girl did have lungs and a heart, but there was no way he could be certain.

He looked into her face, astonished by her beauty. How could the Wildland possibly reproduce such aesthetic perfection? And why should it? He knew, of course, what Okuyama's opinion would be—that the girl was a carefully-designed trap, a beguiling lorelei intended to mesmerise men with lust, clutching them with simulated passion while the Wildland's other agents took advantage of their distraction. Burslem was not so sure. He wondered whether the making of such humanoids might not be a godlike endeavour of creation—the invention of a potentially-intelligent species to complete the Wildland's Eden, to be the mind and soul of its ecosystem. He was not of the party which considered the Wildland intelligent, but he often speculated as to whether the human genetic material taken in by the alien invader when it destroyed all indigenous surface life might enable it eventually to *become* intelligent, or to grant intelligence to some of its motiles.

With his sheathed fingertips he traced the line of her jaw, then drew a line downwards, to the vestigial nipples on her useless breast. He continued, reaching the phantom navel in her abdomen before he suddenly looked up, guiltily, to see that Okuyama had returned with the kit, and was watching him curiously.

"You see," said Burslem, "Adam and Eve might indeed have had navels, although neither was born of woman."

Okuyama scowled, and Burslem realised that the small man was very frightened by what had happened. While he was excited by the unprecedented discovery, Okuyama was in a turmoil of dread, and would not rest easy until this wonderful creature was safe in a sterile tank, ready to be vivisected by careful mechanical manipulators—for such would surely be her fate, if they could get her to the airlocks. For one brief moment, Burslem was sickened by this thought, and tempted to abandon the catch—to let her return to her tree, and be reabsorbed into its flesh, perhaps to be regenerated again, healthy and whole. Then he realised that such an opportunity as this could not be lost, however horrible it would be to turn such beauty over to the investigating thrust of scalpels and syringes.

Burslem stood back, and let Okuyama drag the dead weight of the dryad on to the spread-out plastic tent, roll her up, and seal her tightly within—cut off as completely as they were themselves from the Wildland.

If she did need to breathe, then she would very soon be dead—and this thought too nearly called forth an objection from Burslem, though he strangled the impulse as Okuyama looked up at him again.

"I'll carry her," said Burslem. "You bring the equipment."

"*I'll* carry *it*," Okuyama corrected him. "*You* bring the equipment."

It was Burslem's turn to scowl, but he turned away, and did as he was told. Despite the fact that he was the smaller man, Okuyama seemed to have no difficulty in hoisting the dryad over his shoulder. Together, they set off across a web-like bridge of branches, trying to find a place where they could safely descend to ground level, where they would be able to find a less hazardous path back to the airlocks.

* * *

Okuyama, who led the way, was in a virtual fever of anxious thought. He knew of Burslem's admiring fascination for the alien ecosphere, though he was careful never to argue about it—better, he thought, to let a traitor think that his treason was not discovered. Even before he had seen the lascivious way in which Burslem touched the thing, he had known that Burslem would be taken in by it, would fall in love with it. Burslem was blind to the truth of what this actually was, would think of it as though it were a *person*, would want to defend it against the enquiries to which it would have to be subjected. He must beware of Burslem, be on his guard against any act of treachery.

If necessary, Okuyama thought, *I must be ready to shoot him, in case he should lead us both to our deaths.*

With this thought in mind he was careful to stay behind his companion, keeping the other man under observation. As they made their descent toward the forest floor, he was forced on several occasions to lower the dead weight of the trussed dryad upon a rope, though he did not like to let Burslem handle the thing. More than once he wondered whether it might be sensible to smash the dryad's face with the handle of the drill, to destroy that seductive allure. But he did not do it, because he was a scientist, and it went against the grain to damage a specimen.

He could not help wondering why the Wildland had now begun producing dryads in this region. When the alien spores had seeded the planet, the tripartite division had already taken place, and there were no men on the surface outside the tropics. In the past, the Wildland had produced its humanoids only in those regions where it had found and absorbed human beings. This humanoid did not seem to be modelled on any tropical race, and he wondered whether the Wildland had taken its genetic inspiration from those luckless Scientific Officers who had come up from the underworld never to return.

Okuyama began to look more closely at the dryad's features, wondering if there was some hint of Rogulski there, or of anyone else he had known—but in fact he had never known any real human being quite so handsome. It had not the paleness of the citizens of Chicago, and it was so very smooth, so perfect in its symmetry. He could not help but wonder whether a man actually could have sexual intercourse with such a creature—whether the slit between its legs gave access to a cavity, or whether it was merely an imitative fold in the skin. He tried to put such thoughts deliberately out of his mind, because he knew that the Wildland had created this monster in order to put them there, but that knowledge was itself a guarantee that the thoughts kept returning.

As the day wore on, the burden became very cumbersome, but he refused to give way to the temptation to turn it over to his more muscular companion, because he was afraid of what might develop if he did.

* * *

When Burslem realised that Okuyama was determined to keep him away from the dryad, he was angry. He was insulted by the other's lack of trust, annoyed by the foolishness which made the little man stagger on even when it was clear that he was overburdened, and distressed by the fact that he was denied the opportunity to exercise his curiosity. He wanted to examine the dryad more closely, to find out more about her anatomy, to study her eyes and her breasts, to savour the element of the miraculous in the godlike workings of the alien being which had claimed Earth for its new Eden.

Of course, he told himself, no matter what Okuyama might think, there was nothing of lust in his curiosity. For all the romance in his soul, he was not about to be bewitched by an alien siren. No matter how beautiful she might be, he would not be tempted to trust her to make contact with his own flesh. The Wildland was too greedy for new organic material, and he was not so stupid as to believe that he might be reincarnated—mind and memory intact—as a dryad scion of some lofty forest giant.

Whenever he looked back at Okuyama, resentfully, he was alarmed to see that the other man seemed shifty and furtive. He did not like the way Okuyama clung to his burden, or the way his hands seemed to clutch in a specially intimate fashion at the parts of the humanoid body. His suspicions were aroused long before they reached the ground, when they stopped for the night, but it was when they rested that he really became aware of the extent of Okuyama's paranoia. Okuyama would not move from the side of the corpse—for surely, now, it must be dead—and became agitated if Burslem approached. The small man was so tired that he would not help Burslem build a fire, and though he told Burslem to get some sleep, it was obvious that he did not intend to go to sleep himself

Burslem feared the effect which darkness and sleeplessness might have on a consciousness already tortured by strange fears and desires. He knew that he too would have to stay awake, and be on his guard, lest Okuyama's state of mind should deteriorate still further, and lead to tragedy. It was obvious that this unprecedented disturbance of their routine mission had thrown Okuyama into such a panic that his sanity could no longer be taken for granted.

* * *

When he realised that Burslem did not intend to go to sleep, Okuyama knew that he was in danger. The other man was watching him, carefully but covertly, and Okuyama knew that some vile or dangerous scheme must be hatching in that cunning brain. Despite all his efforts, he had clearly been unable to prevent Burslem from becoming erotically obsessed with their strange captive. What the big man intended to do about it, Okuyama could not guess, but he knew that he must remain alert to any possibility, and that he must be prepared to act if Burslem showed any sign of doing something foolish.

He kept a lamp burning behind and above him, so that by its light he could see the dryad and Burslem. He let his tired limbs relax, but strove to keep his thoughts and senses sharp and clear. He was glad that they would not need to spend another night on the surface—or should not, if they made as much haste as possible in the gloomy morning. Of course, they must not stop to gather samples or to empty the traps which they had set. The dryad was far more important than anything else.

Despite his best efforts, he began to doze off several times, and eventually lost track of the time. Nevertheless, he was sure that he had not actually slept when he was jerked back to awareness by a touch upon his ankle.

At first he thought Burslem must have crept close, but then he realised that it was the dryad that was was moving—writhing slowly and sinuously as it struggled against the plastic sheeting within which it was wrapped. Its eyes were open, and by the bright light of the lamp he could see that they seemed crazed with panic. Its mouth was opening and shutting, as if trying to release a scream, although there was no air to give it force. Its hands, not quite immobilised by the constraining bonds, groped toward his thighs.

His first reaction was one of mingled fear and disgust, and he fought an impulse to leap to his feet and move backwards until he was well out of range of the desperate hands. Then he realised that there was much more at stake than his own instinctive reaction, and he knew that if Burslem were to see the thing like this, *he* might well react with pity, wanting to loosen the bonds that bound the tent about the thing—perhaps even to allow it a little air.

When he looked up, he saw that Burslem was indeed coming forward to see what was happening, with some degree of urgency.

Reflexively, he drew his gun.

* * *

Burslem could not see what had happened to make Okuyama suddenly so agitated, because the lamp was behind Okuyama's head, and the dryad was in his shadow. Nevertheless, he saw the other man jerk convulsively, as if waking from a nightmare, or as if some creeping motile had come to attack him. Whatever it was, though, something had clearly occurred, and Burslem came rapidly to his feet, starting forward so hurriedly that he did not even spare himself the time to ask what was wrong.

When he saw Okuyama go for his gun, he naturally went for his own, but he had hardly got it free from the holster when Okuyama fired.

The bullet went wide, and did not actually touch Burslem's body. He felt only a momentary twitch, as if someone had tried to catch his sleeve, and not quite succeeded. Nevertheless, there was not the slightest doubt in his mind that Okuyama had fired at him, intending to kill, and that the shot had missed only because his own reflexes had betrayed him.

Burslem knew instantly that Okuyama had gone completely mad, and that he must protect himself from the threat of further injury. Even so, he did not want to kill the other man if it could possibly be avoided. He did not fire his own gun, but launched himself instead at his assailant, who had not yet succeeded in raising himself from a sitting position. When he brought his weight down on the body of the smaller man, he succeeded in knocking both of his arms wide, and knocking the wind out of him.

Okuyama did not get the chance to fire a second shot, and Burslem was able to wrench the gun from his fingers and hurl it away. Knowing that the pliant plastic would not break, he brought his own gun down hard on the top of Okuyama's helmet, and he felt the other man go instantly limp beneath him, knocked unconscious.

He breathed out in relief. When daylight came, he thought, he could make Okuyama see sense again, and forget his lunacy long enough to get the dryad back to the airlock and down into Chicago Underground.

It was not until he came to his feet that he realised that although Okuyama was quite still, the dryad was not.

While he stared down at the body, still struggling against its restraints, he put his hand up reflexively to scratch an itch on his upper arm.

When he felt the edges of the tear which the bullet had ripped in his suit, he knew that he was in far worse trouble than he had thought. The Wildland's tiniest agents could reach him even through the smallest of tears.

He turned around quickly, dropping to his knees to search through the packs he had carried all day, desperate to find a sealant that would close the rip in his suit, hoping that he might, by some miracle, be just in time to save himself.

Just as he found the tube of sealant, though, he felt something coil around his wrist and clamp it tight. It was only a bowerconstrictor, and would normally have been no serious threat, but in the present situation, any delay at all might prove fatal. While he wrestled with the thing, he realised that the fire was burning too low, and that the air was suddenly full of insectiles, swooping about him almost as if they had been summoned.

As he began to flail about him with his free hand, he felt the panic rising in his blood, and he knew that the Wildland had him at last, and could do with him whatever it wished.

* * *

When Okuyama woke, it was long after dawn. Even here, in the depths of dense forest, a little sunlight crept through the layers of the canopy. It was perhaps as well, because the lamp which had been behind him was no longer burning.

At first, as he raised his head, blinking his eyes and trying to peer into the gloom, he could not remember what had happened. Then, as a blinding shock of pain made him shut his eyes, it came back to him. Burslem, seeing that the dryad was not dead after all, had come at him, and had gone for his gun. He had tried to drive him back with a warning shot, but the poor fool had come so fast that he was not even certain that he had been able to fire wide—and then that massive body had squashed him flat, and he had struck his head . . . which now felt as if it had been split apart.

With his hand on his forehead, and trying hard not to move, Okuyama forced his eyes open again, determined to see what there was to be seen.

He began immediately to wish that he had not awakened so soon.

The dryad, no longer swaddled in the tent and bound tightly about, was some three metres away. She had her back to him, and could not have seen him anyhow, but he guessed from her attitude that her attention was fully taken up by what she was doing. She was kneeling astride a supine human form, moving rhythmically, her head thrown back as if she were entranced.

He judged from the urgency of her motions that the act of intercourse was coming rapidly to its climax, and he judged that he had very little time in which to act, but his gun was no longer in his hand, and was nowhere close by. Because he had carried the dryad while Burslem had carried the rest of the heavy equipment, there was nothing else immediately to hand which he could use as a weapon, and so he was bare-handed when he came to his feet.

Despite the pain in his head he lurched desperately toward the oblivious couple, cursing Burslem for the appalling weakness which had made him such a ready and stupid victim of the Wildland. He grabbed the dryad around the neck, and yanked her savagely backwards, as if he thought that there might be some slight chance of saving Burslem if only he could interrupt the unnatural congress before its reached its climax. He tried to establish a strangling grip, or one which might have enabled him to break her neck if she had humanoid vertebrae, but he was not strong enough, and he realised that she was neither so small nor so frail as she had been when they had captured her.

He felt stupidly weak as she turned within his hold to grapple with him, and even without the injury to his head she would have been the stronger. She was much bigger now than she had been when he had been able to carry her, and he thought for a moment that this must be a different dryad—but when he saw her face he knew that it was not.

He wished, desperately, that he had tried to find the gun instead of launching himself into what had turned out to be a ridiculously ineffectual attack. He lay on his back, staring up into her wide-eyed face, which was still very beautiful despite the fact that it now had dimensions almost twice as great as it had had when last he had looked into those features.

She smiled, and he had to turn away, looking toward the body of the other man which she had so recently sat astride. That body, stripped of most of its flesh as well as its plastic suit, was grotesquely crumpled and molten.

"Poor Burslem," he whispered. "I knew, you see . . . "

But there was no point in explaining. She had no thoughts of her own, no desires, no feelings. She could not know how she had tempted Burslem, and driven him mad. It was merely her nature, to draw men to damnation, and she could not understand what it was that she did, or how, or why.

When she began to explore, with fingers that were big and clumsy now, the fastenings which sealed his suit, he knew that he had only a limited time to live before he too was consumed by that absurd parody of love-making . . . just as all that fraction of Earth's biosphere which had remained on the surface after the tripartite division had been consumed in equally strange rituals.

"You can never win," he told her. "Because men like me will never yield to your seductions. You may rape us, one by one, but you can never utterly destroy us, because we cannot be fooled. We cannot be tricked into helping you, as poor Burslem was. The Burslems you will always conquer, but the Okuyamas you never can, for we are the true men, and we will always see you for what you really are."

And yet, despite his resolution, his courage, and his knowledge of the truth, when she finally began to draw him into her body, he could not help feeling that this was where he had always truly belonged.

Printed in the United States
1222200002B/112